The Wild Cat Crime

Prince roared, the sound ripping through the night. Fear shot through Nancy. Her gaze swept the foliage around her. Once more the cougar cried out, but she couldn't pinpoint the location. The noise seemed to rise from the entire habitat.

Just then, about forty feet away, the moonlight glanced off a pair of wild-looking yellow eyes. It was Prince, stalking her from a cluster of trees.

Prince stared at Nancy for a moment, then leaped forward. Desperately, Nancy swiveled around and hugged the wall, knowing there was no way she could outrun him. She braced herself, expecting at any moment to feel the claws of the big animal tearing through her skin. . . .

Nancy Drew Mystery Stories

#57 The Triple Hoax
#58 The Flying Saucer Mystery
#62 The Kachina Doll Mystery
#63 The Twin Dilemma
#67 The Sinister Omen
#68 The Elusive Heiress
#70 The Broken Anchor
#72 The Haunted Carousel
#73 Enemy Match
#76 The Eskimo's Secret
#77 The Bluebeard Room
#78 The Phantom of Venice
#79 The Double Horror of Fenley Place
#81 The Mardi Gras Mystery
#87 The Case of the Rising Stars
#89 The Case of the Disappearing Deejay
#91 The Girl Who Couldn't Remember
#92 The Ghost of Craven Cove
#93 The Case of the Safecracker's Secret
#94 The Picture-Perfect Mystery
#97 The Mystery at Magnolia Mansion
#98 The Haunting of Horse Island
#99 The Secret of Seven Rocks
#101 The Mystery of the Missing Millionairess
#102 The Secret in the Dark
#103 The Stranger in the Shadows
#104 The Mystery of the Jade Tiger
#105 The Clue in the Antique Trunk
#106 The Case of the Artful Crime
#108 The Secret of the Tibetan Treasure
#109 The Mystery of the Masked Rider
#110 The Nutcracker Ballet Mystery
#111 The Secret at Solaire
#112 Crime in the Queen's Court
#113 The Secret Lost at Sea
#114 The Search for the Silver Persian
#115 The Suspect in the Smoke
#116 The Case of the Twin Teddy Bears
#117 Mystery on the Menu
#118 Trouble at Lake Tahoe
#119 The Mystery of the Missing Mascot
#120 The Case of the Floating Crime
#121 The Fortune-Teller's Secret
#122 The Message in the Haunted Mansion
#123 The Clue on the Silver Screen
#124 The Secret of the Scarlet Hand
#125 The Teen Model Mystery
#126 The Riddle in the Rare Book
#127 The Case of the Dangerous Solution
#128 The Treasure in the Royal Tower
#129 The Baby-sitter Burglaries
#130 The Sign of the Falcon
#131 The Hidden Inheritance
#132 The Fox Hunt Mystery
#133 The Mystery at the Crystal Palace
#134 The Secret of the Forgotten Cave
#135 The Riddle of the Ruby Gazelle
#136 The Wedding Day Mystery
#137 In Search of the Black Rose
#138 The Legend of the Lost Gold
#139 The Secret of Candlelight Inn
#140 The Door-to-Door Deception
#141 The Wild Cat Crime

Available from MINSTREL Books

141

THE WILD CAT CRIME

CAROLYN KEENE

J
KEENE

Published by POCKET BOOKS
New York London Toronto Sydney Tokyo Singapore

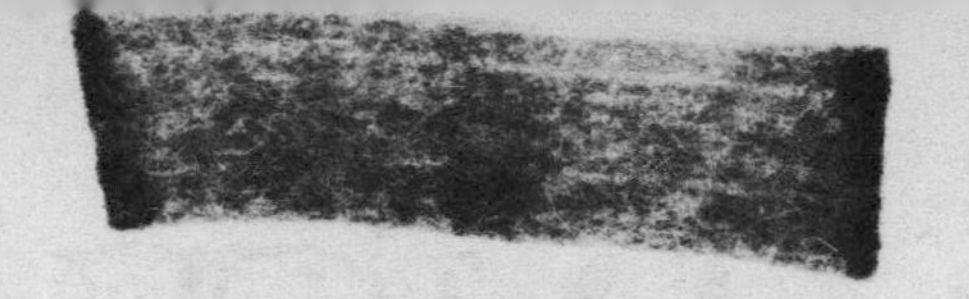

This book is a work of fiction. Names, characters, places and incidents are products of the author's imagination or are used fictitiously. Any resemblance to actual events or locales or persons living or dead is entirely coincidental.

A MINSTREL PAPERBACK *Original*

A Minstrel Book published by
POCKET BOOKS, a division of Simon & Schuster Inc.
1230 Avenue of the Americas, New York, NY 10020

Produced by Mega-Books, Inc.

ISBN: 0-671-00120-5

First Minstrel Books printing February 1998

10 9 8 7 6 5 4 3 2 1

Cover art by Ernie Norcia

Printed in the U.S.A.

Contents

THE
WILD CAT CRIME

1

Endangered Species

"Wow, Bess, that's fabulous news!" Nancy Drew exclaimed into the phone. Nancy glanced at the clock on her desk in the Channel 9 television newsroom, where she and her friend George Fayne were working as summer interns. "It's nine o'clock now. If Christy okays the job, we'll be at the zoo with a camera crew by ten. See you then."

Nancy hung up the phone, her blue eyes sparkling with excitement. She swiveled her chair toward George, who was sitting cross-legged on top of Nancy's desk, sipping a cup of morning tea.

"What's up, Nan?" George asked. "Did Bess meet a cute guy?"

Nancy laughed. "Get off my desk, George,

then I'll tell you Bess's news. Christy might not like it if she sees one of her interns goofing off."

George rolled her eyes. "Christy hasn't paid any attention to us since we started here last week," she whispered. "I don't think she'd notice if I was standing on my head."

"I know what you mean," Nancy admitted as George hopped down.

Nancy and George had been thrilled when Otto Liski, the news producer at WRVH-TV—which were the call letters of Channel 9—had hired them to be part-time interns. But Christy Kelley, their immediate boss and an investigative reporter for the network, had barely spoken a word to them since they'd arrived.

"So what's Bess's news?" George asked, sitting down in a chair.

Nancy smiled and pulled her shoulder-length reddish blond hair into a ponytail. "Last night Katie, the female cougar at the zoo, gave birth to four cubs. Since cougars are endangered animals, everyone at the zoo is incredibly excited about them. Bess thought we might want to do a story on them." Bess Marvin was Nancy's other best friend and George's cousin. The week before, Bess had started her summer internship at the River Heights Zoo, working under Sally Nelson, the zoo veterinarian.

"That *is* great news," George said. "But do you think Christy will let us help with the story? She usually wants to do everything herself."

"We'll see," Nancy said, rising. "I'll go look for her."

Nancy threaded her way through rows of desks in the busy newsroom, skirting an editor who was posting story assignments on a chalkboard. At the desks, a number of reporters pounded out stories on computers or talked on the phone. Most of the desks were littered with papers, used coffee cups, and candy-bar wrappers.

Several reporters had dark circles under their eyes, as though they'd been chasing stories far into the night. So far none of the workers had seemed particularly interested in the new interns, Nancy had observed.

A blond woman wearing a beige business suit and black pumps rushed into the newsroom, nearly colliding with Nancy at the door.

"Excuse me, Nancy," the woman said crisply. "I can't talk now. I'm onto a story."

"I've got a story too, Christy," Nancy said. "I was hoping it would interest you."

Christy narrowed her blue eyes at Nancy. "Well, shoot. But it had better be good. I'm very busy."

Christy tapped her foot impatiently as Nancy told her about the birth of the baby cougars. But when Nancy mentioned that cougars were endangered, Christy's interest perked up.

"A perfect story for the evening news!" Christy announced. "I'll send a camera crew immediately."

"George and I would like to help you with the story," Nancy offered. "We have a friend at the zoo who might give us some interesting details."

Christy pursed her lips and adjusted the tortoiseshell headband that held back her shoulder-length hair. "Hmm, let me think. Tom Hawkins, the cameraman, and Joey Zamboni, the soundman, need to go to the zoo right away to shoot B-roll—background film I'll use to flesh out my story. That's enough people for now. We don't want to upset the mother cougar." She cocked her head and looked at Nancy appraisingly. "But who knows? You and George might be useful later. I'll let you know."

Christy dumped some papers on a reporter's desk, then whirled out of the room while Nancy returned to her desk. In a low voice, Nancy told George what Christy had said.

"I wouldn't be surprised if Christy's ignoring us because she's jealous of you," George muttered. "After all, Mr. Liski hired us because of your experience as a detective. Christy seems pretty ambitious. She might be worried you'll do a better job investigating stories."

Although Nancy was only eighteen, she was an accomplished detective who had solved many difficult and dangerous cases. George and Bess had helped her tackle many of them.

Nancy thought about George's comment for a moment. Could Christy really be jealous of me? She doubted that an experienced reporter like

Christy would be so easily threatened. But it was clear to Nancy that Christy resented having assistants whom she hadn't chosen herself.

Once again Christy breezed through the doorway of the newsroom, her heels making staccato clicks on the linoleum floor. A tall, dark-skinned young man trailed after her. He wore khaki pants and a blue cotton shirt with rolled-up sleeves. A friendly smile lit up his handsome face. Nancy recognized him as the WRVH cameraman, Tom Hawkins. Everyone called him Hawk.

"Nancy, George," Christy called, hurrying over to where the girls stood, then stopping abruptly right in front of them. "It turns out I do need your help after all. My workload today is impossible."

"I had this great idea—" Hawk began excitedly, when Christy cut him off.

"Hawk suggested we include a brief photo montage of cougars in the wild with our story," she said. "Would you two be good enough to run over to the library and check out a few magazines with pictures of cougars? And while you're there, I'd like you to do some research on cougars for my presentation—just the basics."

"Sure," Nancy said. She stood up, smoothing her sleeveless black linen blouse and beige slacks.

"Anything you can find out about the species would be great," Christy went on. "Once I get your material, I'll head over to the zoo to tape my stand-up report. I'd like it no later than one o'clock." Without waiting for a reply, Christy turned on her heel and strode out of the newsroom. Hawk shrugged apologetically, then followed.

"Whew," George said. "Was she a drill sergeant in a previous life or something? I feel like I should've saluted. And I wish she'd sent us to the zoo instead of the library."

"At least she's assigned us some work," Nancy pointed out.

"Yeah—we won't have to sit around anymore, sharpening pencils and pretending to be busy," George said. "C'mon, Drew. It's library time."

"That's it for this article." Nancy flipped her magazine closed. She and George were sitting at a table in the periodicals section of the River Heights public library. Several brightly colored magazines were scattered around them. Nancy placed her magazine aside, then opened up another one and peered at the large, glossy pictures of wild cats.

"Look, Nan," George whispered, pointing to a picture in her magazine. "Cougar cubs are a different color from their parents. The mother is plain yellow-brown, but the babies are lighter with big black spots."

"That's interesting." Nancy leaned toward George and studied the picture of two baby cougars being nursed by their mother.

"This says," George went on, "that unlike other wild cats, cougars won't usually attack humans, unless you threaten a mother or her cubs. Then she'll treat you like prey. She'll leap on you, drag you to the ground, and break your neck, not to mention maul you extensively with her claws and teeth for good measure." George glanced at Nancy. "Wow. That's some maternal instinct. They're big animals, you know."

Nancy raised her brows. "I don't think you have to worry. I bet Bess's mother cougar is locked safely behind bars." Nancy jotted down George's information on a piece of yellow lined paper and looked at her watch. "I think we've got enough material for Christy's story. We've gone through several encyclopedias and magazine articles, and it's only eleven-thirty."

"I'm getting a little tired of being inside on this sunny day, anyway," George said, frowning at the fluorescent lights. A soft breeze blew in through an open window. "What do you say we swing by the zoo on our way back to work? I'd like to see those cubs and also say hi to Bess. We can still get this material to Christy by one o'clock."

Nancy slid her pad of paper into a canvas satchel. "Great idea. We also might learn some things from Bess and the vet that we haven't found in a book."

"There's no substitute for the real thing," George agreed. "Let's go."

After noting which magazines had the best pictures, George and Nancy left the library and drove off toward the zoo in Nancy's blue Mustang.

Nancy found a parking space near the entrance. As the girls stepped out of the car, George pulled a maroon baseball cap from her purse and pulled it over her short dark curls. "Christy might not like the look," she commented, "but at least this hat keeps the sun out of my face."

Nancy smiled. George and Bess were so different, she mused. George loved sports and wearing jeans and sneakers, while her cousin Bess preferred boy-watching, hot fudge sundaes, and shopping at the mall. But despite their differences, George and Bess were loyal friends.

Nancy locked her car, and the two girls headed for the zoo entrance. They walked along the eight-foot-high stone wall surrounding the grounds and through the wide-open gates made of iron bars.

The first thing Nancy noticed inside was a monorail track leading to a quaint, old-fashioned-looking train platform and station. It looks like a station where Sherlock Holmes might catch a train, Nancy thought.

After paying their admission fee, the two followed the signs for the cougar habitat. Down a leafy path, which curved past a group of elephants and zebras, Nancy spotted a blond girl sitting on a bench in a patch of sunlight. Her eyes were closed, and her pretty face was tilted dreamily toward the sun.

"Bess!" Nancy shouted. She jogged up to her. "Caught you—asleep on the job."

Bess jolted to attention, then tugged her lavender miniskirt toward her knees. Her blue eyes darted guiltily from Nancy to George. "Uh, hi, guys. I . . . I was just trying to relax. The WRVH camera crew left about an hour ago, and things were really hectic."

"An hour ago?" George exclaimed. "And you've been sitting her all this time? I hope you're wearing sunblock," she chided her cousin, "or you'll be burned to a crisp."

Bess frowned, anxiously poking her cheeks. "Do I look burned? I was trying to catch the perfect tan—for Randy."

"Randy?" Nancy said. "Who's he?"

"Randy Thompson, the assistant vet," Bess gushed. "Wait till you guys see him. He's almost as cute as the baby cougars."

"And much more endangered, if you've got your eye on him," George muttered, looking pointedly at Bess.

Bess shot her cousin a withering look. "If you think I've been hounding Randy, you're totally wrong. He barely knows I exist." Bess suddenly frowned. "Why aren't you guys at work?"

"We are," George said, with a laugh. "It's a tough job, I know."

Nancy gave George a friendly shove for being so silly. "We've been at the library doing cougar research for Christy. We have plenty of time before we have to be back to the station, so we thought we'd stop by."

"To see the cougars, I bet," Bess said.

"And you, too, dear cousin," George added.

"You're just lucky that the little guys are so cute; otherwise, I might be offended. Come on. Their cage is this way. They're inside the nursery next to the cougar habitat."

"Lead on, Bess," Nancy said. She scanned the ten-foot-tall chain-link fence on her right. About twenty feet beyond it, a male lion rested on a rock. His yellow eyes looked proudly around his domain, while a lioness roamed the grassy field below.

"Each cat species has its own bit of land—about two or three acres that resembles the cat's natural habitat so it will feel right at home," Bess explained as they walked along. "The habitats are separated by big moats of water. Most wild cats hate to get wet—just like house cats—so they won't cross the moats."

George smiled. "I'm impressed with how much you know, Bess. I guess you haven't spent *all* your time here sunbathing."

Bess flashed George a sly grin. "I've been doing my homework. I can't have Randy thinking I'm just a dumb blond.

"Here we are," Bess announced, pointing to a

field full of bushes, trees, and rocks. A low stone building with a chain-link fence sprouting from either side stood between the walkway and the habitat. The front of the building had three entrances, and Nancy assumed that the back of the building also had doors, so the cougars could go back and forth, inside and out, as they wished.

Bess opened the nearest door to let them in. "The nursery cage is separated from the others to give Katie and her four cubs some peace and quiet. We're not letting the public in here until the cubs are older—except, of course, for the TV crew this morning."

Inside, there was a small spectator area in front of a large, clean cage with a padlocked gate. Katie, a tawny cougar about five feet long, was asleep in the cage on a thin bed of straw. Snuggling close to her belly were the cubs, all making high-pitched squeaks.

"They're so adorable," Nancy said, admiring the tiny bodies covered with spotted fur. "The way they're squirming, you can't tell where one stops and the next one begins." She tried counting them.

Suddenly, she frowned and quickly scanned the cage. "Didn't you say there were four cubs, Bess?" she asked, her eyes wide.

"Yes," Bess said, staring into the cage. "One, two, three—" She stopped and started counting again. "One, two, three—"

Bess shot Nancy a look of sheer panic.

2

A Clue in the Cage

"One of the cubs is missing!" Bess cried. "What are we going to do?"

"Bess, calm down," George said. "Maybe the vet just took it away for shots or something. You were out sunbathing for an hour."

"Maybe," Bess said. She puckered her brow. "They were all here when I left. You guys stay here—I'll go find Sally." Without waiting for a reply, Bess dashed out of the building.

While Nancy and George waited for Bess to return with the vet, Nancy studied the mother cougar's cage. Its iron bars ran from floor to ceiling, and the door was padlocked shut. Just as Nancy had supposed, there was a door at the back of the cage that led to outdoors. But, of course, it was closed to keep Katie and her cubs safe inside.

Wait a second, Nancy thought. It isn't closed. Nancy could make out a sliver of light between the door and the jamb. Maybe the missing cougar cub had crawled outside.

Nancy carefully scanned the cage again, and this time she noticed something glistening in the straw. Pressing her face against the bars, she strained to see what it was.

Just then she heard one of the front doors open and she spun around to see a young woman with shoulder-length dark hair rush into the nursery. Bess was two steps behind the woman, her face pale.

"Sally says she doesn't have the cub at the infirmary," Bess announced. "It's missing."

Nancy studied the tall, dark-haired woman. On her khaki zoo uniform was a name badge that read "Sally Nelson, DVM." Nancy knew the initials stood for Doctor of Veterinary Medicine.

"The back door of Katie's cage is ajar," Nancy told the vet. "Is it usually left open like that?"

Sally glanced toward the back door, then took a key ring from her pocket. "No," she answered. "But there must be some explanation for why it's open now. I'll go check out the habitat."

Nancy, George, and Bess followed Sally outside to a gate in the fence that enclosed the habitat. From where she stood, Nancy could see most of the habitat, except for the area directly behind the nursery building. There was no sign of the cub anywhere.

As Sally unlocked the padlock on the gate, she said, "Wait here. I'm familiar to Katie, but if she sensed the presence of strangers, she might wake up and feel threatened." She slipped through the gate and fastened the lock behind her.

Nancy watched as Sally disappeared around the back of the building. Almost instantly, Sally came back into view—with a cougar cub cradled in her arms.

"Oh, thank goodness." Bess took a deep breath.

"Where was it?" George asked.

"He was lying just outside the door leading from the nursery cage to the habitat," Sally explained. She came back through the gate and locked it up again.

Nancy, George, and Bess gathered around her and the little cougar. Sally nuzzled it against her cheek, her large green eyes gazing at it warmly. "You've been a naughty boy," she said, "making us all worry like that. You nearly gave Bess a heart attack."

Bess blushed. "I thought I did pretty well, considering. . . ."

"You handled the situation perfectly, Bess," Sally said. "You were right to be concerned when you couldn't find the cub. I was worried, too. But now that's over. Why don't you introduce me to your friends?"

Bess introduced Nancy and George to Sally and explained that her friends were interns at WRVH.

Sally looked at Nancy and George curiously. "I met your colleagues here this morning—a guy named Hawk and his friend Joey."

"Hawk and Joey came over to do the background film," Nancy said. "Our boss, Christy, is planning to stop by later to tape her story on the cougars for the evening news."

"So I hear," Sally said. "All that commotion this morning must have given this little guy a start," she added, stroking the cougar. "I can't believe he wandered so far from his mom, especially when he hasn't even opened his eyes yet."

"Is he okay?" Nancy asked. She guessed the cub probably weighed about a pound. Like the picture of the cougar cubs in the library, it was tan with dark spots. Around its short tan tail were several dark rings.

"He seems fine," Sally replied. She held up the cub and peered into his face. "Except we may need to feed him some milk—he probably hasn't nursed for a while, and I'm worried he might get pushed out of the way by his stronger siblings."

Nancy felt relieved that the cougar was safe and healthy. Still, she shared Sally's puzzlement that the cub had wandered so far away from his mother.

"Would he have the strength to push that door open on his own?" Nancy asked.

Sally cast her eyes down toward the cub in her arms. She blew softly on him, creating a slight ripple in the cub's fur. Was it Nancy's imagination, or did Nancy detect a flicker of unease in Sally's expression?

"The space wasn't big enough for him to crawl through," Sally admitted. "And I don't think he'd have the strength to push it open any farther."

Nancy nodded, watching Sally carefully as she sighed.

"What bothers me," Sally went on, "is that the door is usually kept closed and locked." She gave Nancy a troubled look. "Maybe someone wasn't thinking and left it open—possibly Junior Anderson. He's the man who feeds the animals and cleans their cages. The cub might have crawled outside while Junior was cleaning the cage."

"But once he'd finished, wouldn't he have noticed the little cougar outside the door and put it back with Katie?" George asked.

Sally didn't answer. She looked thoughtfully down at the cub. After a moment, she said, "Junior is an elderly man and his eyesight isn't so great. It's possible he just didn't see the cub." She paused, then continued, "This cub is the runt of the litter. I wonder if Katie could have rejected him—that sometimes happens with wild animals."

"But all four cubs were nursing just fine when I

checked just a little over an hour ago," Bess pointed out.

Sally shrugged. "The only explanation I can think of is that this guy is extra ambitious and crawled out the nursery door when Junior came along to feed Katie."

"Well, whatever happened, at least everything's okay now," Bess said brightly. "That's the important thing." She reached forward and scratched the cub under its chin.

"Wise words, Bess," Sally said. "Now, if you girls will excuse me for a moment, I'm going to get him some milk. There's a bottle in the infirmary fridge with your name on it, little guy." Sally bent toward the cub and smiled, her dark hair sweeping over the cub's scruffy light brown baby fur.

Sally set off for the infirmary, cradling the cougar in her arms.

Nancy waited until Sally was out of sight, then motioned for Bess and George to follow her back into the nursery building.

"See that glittery thing in Katie's cage?" she said, pointing to a spot in the straw across the cage from the sleeping Katie. "I wonder what it is."

"Only one way to find out," George said gamely. She tossed Nancy a broom, which had been propped against the wall.

"Thanks, Fayne," Nancy said, grinning. "Would you guys guard the entrance? It's not that I don't trust Sally, but I'm not ready to let her in on every clue I find."

George and Bess walked out the front door they'd just come through, to take up their lookout posts.

Nancy double-checked to make sure that Katie was still asleep before she poked the bristle end of the broom through the cage bars. Stretching as far as she could, she was just able to reach the glittery object. She held her breath for a moment. Nancy didn't want to push the object farther back by mistake or drop the broom, but she had to hurry. She had no idea when Sally might return.

She inched the broom a little bit farther and just barely touched the object. Making small sweeping motions toward herself, Nancy carefully guided the object close to the front of the cage. When the object was about a foot and a half away from her, Nancy glanced once more at the huge animal asleep at the other end of the cage. Katie hadn't stirred. Quickly, Nancy reached through the bars and grabbed the shiny object with her hand.

With a sigh of relief, Nancy sat back on her heels and peered at the object nestled in her palm. It was a heavy gold ring—a man's ring—with a bird engraved on it. A memory tugged at her mind. I've seen this ring before, she thought, but where?

Nancy slipped the ring into the pocket of her

pants. Then she put the broom back where George had found it and stepped outside into the sunlight.

Nancy took a good look around. Bess and George were chatting a few feet away by the chain-link fence. About fifty feet away, Nancy could see the top of a concession stand. Its yellow- and white-striped canvas top looked festive in the shade of a large maple tree. There was no sign of Sally. She walked over to join her friends.

"Hey, Nan," George said. "What did you find?"

Nancy reached into her pocket and enclosed the ring in her fist. She brought it out and opened her palm. The ring shone in the bright sun.

"That looks like a hawk engraved on it," George commented.

Nancy frowned, thinking. "You're right." She tilted the ring to study the inside. The letters T. H. were engraved on the inner band. Someone's initials, she guessed, but whose?

In a flash, Nancy remembered where she had seem the ring before: on the hand of the cameraman at WRVH, Hawk. His real name was Tom Hawkins. That explained both the engraved hawk and the initials.

Nancy slipped the ring back into her pocket, her mind in a whirl. "It's Hawk's ring," she said to George. "But what could he have been doing inside the cougar's locked cage?"

3

Ready to Strike

George looked stunned. "You think Hawk went inside Katie's cage?"

But before Nancy could reply, Bess called their attention to the cougar habitat.

"Look," she said, her voice a mixture of excitement and awe. "Here comes Prince. Isn't he a gorgeous animal?" She pointed to a large cougar standing in the shade of a hemlock tree about fifty feet away.

"He sure is," Nancy agreed.

"And huge!" George exclaimed.

"He's Katie's mate, the cubs' father," Bess informed them. She cocked her head as she gazed at the majestic animal. "I feel sorry for him, though. Katie and the cubs have been getting all the attention. He's looking kind of forlorn."

"Then why don't you go in and give him a hug?" George teased. "I'm sure it would warm his heart."

"No thanks!" Bess said, giving George a playful punch. "I'm not into human sacrifice."

"I thought cougars were supposed to be less dangerous than other big cats," Nancy said. As she spoke, Prince tilted his head toward his audience and roared, his amber eyes fixed upon them.

Bess jumped. "Yikes!"

Nancy and George laughed, and a voice shouted out behind them, "Oh, Prince, stop that. Mind your manners."

Turning, Nancy saw Sally approaching again. She was feeding the cougar cub with a bottle, like a human baby.

"They look like gorgeous, giant house cats, don't they?" Sally asked, as if she had just heard George tease Bess about hugging Prince. "Cougars can be playful with people they know, but they're still wild animals," she explained. "I would never advise an inexperienced person to go anywhere near one. I approach them cautiously. Even Eduardo is careful."

"Eduardo?" Nancy said. "Who's he?"

"Eduardo Vallejo, the cat keeper and trainer at the zoo," Sally replied. "He used to be a lion trainer in the circus. All the big cats respect him. Still, he's on his guard with them—as any professional would be—because he knows how deadly wild cats can be when they're provoked."

"It's hard to believe this cub will one day be a fierce predator," Nancy said, smiling down at the cat in Sally's arms.

Sally laughed. "It's amazing how fast they grow. Here, do you want to hold him for a moment, Nancy?"

"You sure Katie won't mind?" Nancy said. Sally answered by putting the cougar in Nancy's arms. The cub's fuzzy coat felt soft against Nancy's skin. She steadied the bottle in his mouth, and he made greedy, slurping noises as he sucked down the milk.

"I'd worry more about Prince being jealous right now," George said, nodding at the large male pacing near the tree. His eyes stayed focused on them.

Nancy laughed a little nervously. "I think I'd like to stay on both parents' good sides," she said.

"Good thinking," Sally began. "And I'd better be getting this guy back to his mother if I want to stay in her good graces. Wild cats need time together with their babies to bond with them, just as humans do. If Katie *did* reject him," she went on, "we'll need to work extra hard at getting them back together."

Nancy carefully placed the cougar in Sally's arms.

"Do you mind if I ask you a few questions before we go, Sally?" Nancy asked. She glanced at her watch. "We're due back at the station soon, but I'm still curious about a couple of things about the cub getting outside."

"I'll bet Nancy suspects foul play," Bess blurted out. "She's a detective, and that's the way her mind thinks."

Nancy frowned at Bess. She actually *had* been wondering whether the cougar had been moved from Katie on purpose. If Nancy was right, she certainly didn't want Sally to be on guard around her as she investigated. She—or anyone else at the zoo—could be a suspect.

"Foul play?" Sally asked. "Whatever do you mean?" She addressed her words to Bess, but it was Nancy she looked at in puzzlement.

"Well, uh, just that Nancy might have thought the cougar was moved on purpose," Bess stammered. She shot Nancy a look, and Nancy could tell that Bess regretted her hasty words.

"And do you think that, Nancy?" Sally asked.

"Honestly, Sally, I'm not sure," Nancy replied. "It seems like a stretch that the cougar could have crawled outside on his own, especially when the door is normally locked. Could someone have been trying to take him?"

Sally shivered, and her face grew pale. Light freckles that Nancy hadn't noticed before stood out starkly on her cream-colored skin. "I hope not. That's a dreadful thought. Of course, there *is* a black market for endangered species. A cougar could bring a lot of money."

So someone could have tried to steal the cougar for profit, Nancy thought, mentally filing away the information. Aloud, she asked, "Who else has keys to Katie's cage besides you and Junior Anderson?"

Sally fingered her own keys as she thought. "Hmm. Richard Annenberg has keys, of course. He's the director of the zoo. Then Randy Thompson, my assistant. Eduardo Vallejo, the cat trainer I mentioned. All of us have keys to all the locks on the zoo premises."

"Were you with the camera crew the whole time they were in with the cougars?" Nancy asked, fingering Hawk's gold ring in her pocket.

"Not the whole time," Sally said. "The crew was still filming the cubs from the spectator area right outside the nursery cage when Richard Annenberg called me into his office for a meeting."

"So you don't know how much longer the film crew stayed?" Nancy asked.

"I happened to look out the window in Richard's office as they were leaving," Sally replied. "I saw them carrying all their gear. I'm not entirely sure, but I'd guess they left about fifteen minutes after I last saw them at the nursery."

Nancy was trying to figure out whether Hawk would have had enough time to go inside the cage and try to take the cougar. Fifteen minutes, she mused, would have been enough time if he had a key to the cage. But how would he have gotten a key? Could he have stolen one?

"After the film crew left," Sally went on, "Richard and I spent about half an hour planning the zoo's museum events. I was on my way back to check on the cubs when I ran into Bess."

"I hate to interrupt, Nan," George said. She pointed to her watch. "But it's already twelve-fifteen, and we have to get back to give Christy our research notes on cougars. We don't want to mess up the first real job that Christy's given us."

"That's for sure," Nancy agreed. "We'd better get going." Turning back to Sally, she added, "Thanks for answering my questions—and for letting me hold the cub. He's adorable. And don't worry—I'm sure everything will be fine."

"I hope so," Sally said.

They all said their good-byes and Bess followed Sally back into the cougar nursery while Nancy and George headed for the main gates of the zoo.

Along the way, George said, "What I'd like to know is, if Hawk *was* the one who moved the cub, how did he avoid getting eaten by Katie?"

"Maybe she was asleep," Nancy suggested. "Or maybe someone else from the zoo moved the cougar. I'd like to stay to do some more investigating, but Christy needs our research notes. Then we'll probably be busy at the station all afternoon getting ready for this story."

George made a face. "Don't count on it. Christy will probably forget about us as usual."

"I hope she does this time," Nancy remarked. "Then maybe I can sneak back here."

As they approached the zoo entrance, a familiar figure rushed toward them.

"Nancy, George!" Hawk shouted. His eyes darted wildly around the zoo, and beads of perspiration lined his forehead. "What are you doing here?" he asked in a panicky voice.

"Just visiting Katie," Nancy began.

"I lost my ring," Hawk said, ignoring Nancy's words. "I can't believe it. My parents gave it to me for college graduation last year. If I don't find it . . ."

"Is this your ring, Hawk?" Nancy asked, holding it out to him. "I found it in the nursery cage." She watched him carefully to see his reaction.

Hawk's face broke into a grin as he took the ring from Nancy and placed it on his finger. "You found it, Nancy! Thank you so much. It's really too loose for my finger. It must have fallen off during the shoot." He thrust his hand in front of his face and looked at the ring with both relief and happiness.

"Do you know what the ring was doing inside the—" Nancy began.

Suddenly, Hawk threw his arms around her, cutting her off in midsentence. "I can't thank you enough, Nancy," he said as he hugged her. "You've saved me." Nancy barely had time to absorb what was happening when Hawk released her. "See you later," he said, then turned and strode toward the gates.

"Wait, Hawk," Nancy called out. "I want to ask you some questions."

"Track me down at the station," Hawk said over his shoulder. "I'm in a crunch getting ready for Christy's story." He jogged through the open gates.

"Whew," George said, a surprised look on her face. "That guy's like a steamroller. He hardly gave us a chance to say a word."

"I wanted to ask him if he knew how his ring had gotten inside Katie's cage, but he cut me off," Nancy remarked. "I wonder if he meant to ignore me."

"Either that, or he wasn't paying attention. He was awfully relieved to have his ring back," George said.

"He sure seemed excited—overly excited, if you ask me," Nancy commented. "It was as though he was putting on a performance."

The sharp smell of mustard and hot dogs wafted through the air around them and set Nancy's stomach rumbling. "Let's grab a hot dog, George," she suggested, pointing to a concession stand by the zoo entrance. "It's lunchtime, and I'm starved."

"Good idea," George said. "We can eat on the way back to the station."

After paying for hot dogs and lemonade, Nancy and George hurried toward the Mustang.

Nancy set her lemonade cup down on the hood while she took her keys from her purse. Suddenly she froze.

Out of the corner of her eye, she saw a strange black object coiled on the roof of her car.

Suddenly, a flared head rose up from it. Nancy gasped. It was a snake—a cobra!

The snake's forked tongue darted in and out of its mouth. It was about to strike!

4

A Mysterious Shadow

"Don't move!" Nancy whispered.

George stopped in her tracks near the passenger-side door, her face frozen in a look of horror. "It's a snake!" she gasped.

The snake responded with a hiss, its tongue flickering in the sun.

Nancy knew that if they made the slightest move, the snake would strike faster than they could run. Nancy resisted the urge to cry out. She remembered reading that there was a way to grab a poisonous snake so it wouldn't bite, but she couldn't remember exactly what it was. She didn't want to risk grabbing the cobra the wrong way.

Nancy looked at the snake guardedly. It stared

back at her, its spade-shaped head weaving back and forth.

No way, Drew, she thought. That snake looks way too mad for you to get anywhere near it, much less grab it. Cobras, she knew, were deadly. If the snake bit her, she could die within minutes.

Out of the corner of her eye, Nancy saw Sally Nelson walking toward them, wearing large gloves and carrying a metal box, which looked like a small animal carrier.

Nancy resisted the urge to cry out, but Sally seemed to be heading straight for them anyway. Nancy held her breath as Sally walked carefully and methodically up to the car.

The vet smoothly raised a finger to her lips to signal that the girls stay quiet. She set the box on the ground with the same graceful movement.

Suddenly, with one deft move, Sally grabbed the snake firmly around its flared head with both hands and held it at arm's length.

Nancy watched the cobra writhe back and forth, lashing its tail as it fought to get free. Sally's arm muscles tightened as she struggled to keep her grip on the snake and prevent it from biting her. In its frenzy, the cobra hissed, its tongue darting about like a tiny streak of lightning.

Finally, the snake seemed to relax, and Sally quickly placed its limp body inside the metal box. Then she shut the lid and clicked the locks shut. "Gotcha, Stanley," she said triumphantly.

"Wow!" George exclaimed. "You were amazing, Sally. I don't know what we would have done if you hadn't come along."

Nancy nodded, her heart still thumping furiously inside her chest. "That was quite a struggle between you and the snake," she said. "I couldn't think what to do."

"You did just the right thing, standing totally still," Sally told them. She stopped and shook her head, looking a little shaken herself.

Nancy could imagine what Sally was thinking. She herself shivered as she thought of their narrow brush with the lethal reptile.

"How did you know we were in trouble?" George asked, casting her eyes toward Sally's gloves and the carrier. "You certainly came prepared."

For the first time, Nancy noticed that Sally was wearing a baseball cap. Sally took off the blue cap and placed it on George's curls. "I'd just found your cap in the nursery, George, when Stanley was discovered missing from his cage at the infirmary."

Sally leaned her face against her hand and rubbed her temple tiredly. "While I was searching for Stanley, I spotted you guys leaving the zoo," she went on, "so I followed you to the car to return the hat. The rest is history. Of course," she added with a wry smile, "I had no idea I was about to save you guys from a life-or-death encounter with a deadly cobra."

"Was Stanley sick?" Nancy asked. "Is that why he was in the infirmary?"

"He had a cut on his tail," Sally explained. "But it was almost healed. We were planning to return him to the reptile house tomorrow morning."

George asked, "So Stanley crawled all the way from the infirmary to the car? That's pretty amazing."

"The zoo is about fifty acres, and the infirmary is in the middle of it. Stanley could have crawled that far, especially because his tail had basically healed, but I don't think he could have crawled onto the roof of the car." Sally frowned, then added, "Plus, I would think that someone would have seen him. After all, he doesn't look like your typical zoo visitor."

"If he couldn't have crawled onto my car by himself, then someone must have planted him there," Nancy reasoned.

Sally looked at Nancy, surprised. "I wasn't suggesting that someone planted him on your car, Nancy," she said defensively.

"I know you didn't *say* that," Nancy said calmly. "But you implied it. You said that Stanley couldn't have climbed onto my car by himself."

Sally sighed. "I'm sorry, Nancy. I didn't mean

to snap at you. It's just that I don't know the answer to your question. Weird things have been happening here today. First the cougar, and now Stanley. I don't know what to think, but I can't imagine that someone would have deliberately put Stanley on your car."

"It is pretty bizarre," Nancy agreed, unlocking her car. She thanked Sally for rescuing them and asked her to let her know if anything else unusual happened at the zoo.

"I sure will," Sally promised. Then she smiled. "Especially now that I know you're a detective." She hefted the metal box and turned back toward the zoo.

As George strapped on her seat belt, she craned her neck around toward the backseat. "Just checking to make sure there aren't any boa constrictors back there," she joked wryly.

"I think we're safe, George—for a while, at least," Nancy said grimly.

"What do you mean, 'for a while'?" George asked nervously.

Nancy hesitated before she answered. She turned on the ignition and then pulled the car onto the busy street. "There's no way Stanley slithered on top of my car on his own," she said firmly. "Someone put him there to warn me to stop my investigation. I wasn't completely sure I had one yet. There still could have been some reasonable explanations for the missing cub and

Hawk's ring, but whoever put that snake here just confirmed that there is indeed a mystery to investigate."

Fifteen minutes later Nancy guided the Mustang into the WRVH parking lot and parked next to Hawk and Joey's news van.

"Hawk's back," George commented. She shot Nancy a look. "He knows what your car looks like. He could have overheard us talking, then put Stanley on the roof of your car."

"It's possible," Nancy said as she and George stepped out of the car. Slinging her purse over her shoulder, Nancy added, "But it's hard to believe that he had enough time to do all that. Plus, why would he want to steal the cougar or try to frighten me?"

"You've got me." George shrugged.

The girls opted for the elevator instead of the stairs to get to the fourth floor of the WRVH building. When the elevator door slid open, Christy was standing in the waiting area directly outside. She stepped back in surprise as Nancy and George got out.

"There you are!" she snapped. "I was beginning to think you girls had gone AWOL. Your research had better be A-plus, that's all I can say."

After handing Christy their material on cougars and assuring her that it was thorough and complete, Nancy and George returned to their desks.

"Hey, hey, girls!" a man's voice called. Nancy looked up to see Joey Zamboni, the dark-haired, easygoing soundman who had worked with Hawk at the zoo. He stood in the doorway of the newsroom, grinning. "It's your lucky day," he said. "Christy has another project for you."

"You're kidding," George replied sarcastically.

"What is it, Joey?" Nancy asked.

"She wants you guys to scan the B-roll from the zoo this morning and find some good shots for her story."

Nancy and George exchanged looks of surprise.

"Are you sure she wants *us*?" Nancy asked.

"That's what the boss lady told me," Joey replied. "Right this way."

He ushered Nancy and George into an editing room and introduced them to Linda Wong, one of the film editors at WRVH. Joey ducked out of the room as Linda turned out the lights and popped the tape into a large machine with a control panel and a monitor.

Nancy and George watched the footage of the newborn cougars on the monitor screen. There were several close-ups of individual cubs, eyes closed and bodies wiggling toward Katie as they attempted to nurse. This time, Katie was awake, her eyes gazing calmly into the camera.

The camera drew back for a long shot, which showed the back wall and door of the nursery cage. Nancy noticed that the back door was closed, just as Sally had said it should be. Nancy kept her eyes riveted on the door as the footage continued to roll.

Suddenly, Nancy blinked. Was the door opening a crack? she wondered. And was that a shadow falling across it? Leaning forward, Nancy peered into the screen. The shadow retreated, and the door shut once more.

Who was that person? she wondered. Who was trying to sneak into Katie's cage?

5

Disaster at the Zoo

As Nancy stared at the screen, she suddenly heard a footstep behind her. Startled, she whirled around.

"Hey, it's just me, Nancy," Joey said, and grinned. "Must be a pretty interesting B-roll to absorb you guys so much."

"I've been totally caught up in it, I admit," Nancy said carefully. The screen went blank as the film ended. The lights came on, and a soft whirring noise filled the room as Linda rewound the tape.

"I have a question for you, Joey," Nancy continued. "Did Hawk ever go into the cage with the cougars while you guys were there?"

Joey looked at Nancy incredulously. "Are you kidding?"

"It does look like some of this film footage is shot from pretty close up," George mused aloud. Nancy wasn't sure if George had noticed the shadow.

"Well, Hawk would never get into a cage with a mother cougar and her cubs," Joey said, shaking his head. "I mean, let's face it: the guy's not an idiot. Those close-ups were all shot from outside the cage, believe me. Hawk aimed the lens between the bars and focused the camera from there."

Nancy thought for a moment. If Hawk had shot every frame of the B-roll, then it wasn't his shadow on the film. But what if he'd taken a break and someone else had filmed that final shot? "Were you with Hawk every moment?" Nancy asked. "Did Hawk ever leave by himself, even for just a few minutes? Did he go to the bathroom or get something to eat while you waited with the equipment?"

Joey's face blanched, and he stared wide-eyed at Nancy. Then he abruptly cast his gaze downward. "Not that I remember," he mumbled.

Nancy frowned. Joey's response struck her as strange.

"There's a shot in the B-roll I'd like you to see, Joey," Nancy said. She asked Linda to replay the end of the film.

As the scene unfolded again, George said, "Whoa, the back door to the cage is opening.

And look—there's a shadow! I didn't notice it the first time."

"It *is* a shadow," Joey commented, surprised. "Could it be the father cougar, Prince?"

"No way. It looks like someone's arm," Nancy declared. "You never noticed the door opening while you guys were shooting? Or the shadow?"

"No," Joey said, shaking his head emphatically. "I don't remember seeing any of that stuff at all. I'm surprised I didn't notice it," he mused with a puzzled air. "After all, I never left the nursery—not once."

Nancy was silent. She had a distinct feeling that Joey knew more than he was telling. He had acted jittery when she'd asked whether Hawk had left the nursery. Could Joey be covering up for Hawk? she wondered. She made up her mind to question Hawk as soon as she had a free moment.

"Uh, I've g-got to go," Joey stammered. "See you guys later." He slipped out of the editing room before Nancy could protest.

Nancy and George went through the B-roll one more time to pick out the best shots for Christy. By the time they had finished, it was already two-thirty.

Nancy went to look for Hawk while George took the edited B-roll to Christy. Ten minutes later the two girls were back at their desks in the newsroom.

"I couldn't find Hawk anywhere," Nancy said. "I'd really like to ask him some questions about what his ring was doing in the cougars' cage."

George nodded. "But why would he want to steal a cougar cub?" she said, repeating the question that Nancy had been thinking over ever since she had found Hawk's ring.

"Beats me," Nancy admitted, rubbing her bare arms in the chilly air-conditioned room. She reached into a desk drawer and took out a baggy cotton sweater. "Somehow Hawk doesn't strike me as the type to climb a chain-link fence and risk facing a wild cougar."

"Maybe he likes the idea of having an exotic pet," George suggested. "He might think dogs and cats are boring."

Nancy shrugged. "Sally did say something about a black market for cougars. It seems far-fetched, but I guess Hawk could be involved in something like that."

"By the way, did you notice that whoever opened the back door in the film shut it again?" George said. "So how did it end up ajar when we were there?"

"Exactly what I've been wondering, George." Nancy pursed her lips as her mind ran over the morning's events. After a moment she added, "Maybe Junior Anderson, the man who feeds the animals, could answer some of these questions."

"You should probably talk to everyone who has

a key, Nan," George pointed out. "Maybe one of them forgot to lock up the nursery cage."

"True," Nancy agreed. "Remember the cat keeper Sally mentioned—Eduardo Vallejo? I definitely want to talk to him about what would make a mother cougar reject her cub. Would she bother to move it outside the door when she's so busy nursing the others?"

"Not to mention that she'd have to open the door first, too," George added.

Nancy nodded. "I've been thinking about Sally ever since she rescued us from that snake. My gut feeling is she's trustworthy, and we should probably tell her about the shadow on the B-roll so she can safeguard the cubs. What if someone was sneaking in to take the cub and got surprised by Joey and Hawk?"

Christy appeared in the doorway of the newsroom, scowling. "Hey, girls, where have you been? You were supposed to be out by the elevators five minutes ago."

"We were?" George said, puzzled. "No one told us."

"Oh, come on," Christy said. "I just told you to meet us there when you handed me the B-roll, George."

Nancy and George exchanged glances. "No way," George mouthed silently to Nancy. Aloud she said, "Sorry, Christy. What is it we're supposed to be doing?"

Christy rolled her eyes. "If you want to succeed in this business, George, you've got to pay attention. Anyway, we're heading over to the zoo right now in my car to tape my stand-up report. Hawk and Joey have already left to set up."

"Back to the zoo?" Nancy said. She and George grabbed their purses and followed Christy out the newsroom door.

By the elevator Christy thrust some papers at Nancy. "Here are your notes from the library," Christy announced. "I want you girls to take a look at these and prompt me if I need more information on cougars. We'll rehearse my piece once we get there." She pressed the elevator button impatiently. "I wish we'd never moved into this new building—the elevators take forever."

Down on the street, they all piled into Christy's cherry red sedan. Nancy opened her backseat window. The warm afternoon sun felt hot after the climate-controlled cold office. Nancy pulled off her sweater and stuffed it into her big purse.

Christy parked in a special visitors' lot close to the zoo entrance. Marching two steps ahead of Nancy and George, she led them down the sidewalk toward the zoo gates. "I'm worried we're late," Christy said to no one in particular. "We *must* get this story back to the station and edited in time for the evening news."

She strode through the gates, then stopped

abruptly. Nancy stumbled up against her. "Sorry, Christy," Nancy said, drawing away. Christy paid no attention—she was staring at something ahead.

A tall middle-aged man sprinted up to them, his black hair flying loose from its ponytail. Despite the hot summer day, the man wore baggy corduroy pants, and a shirttail from his white button-down shirt fluttered around his chubby waist. Wire-rimmed glasses hung crookedly from the tip of his nose. His breath came in short gasps, and his gaze darted frantically around the group.

What's this man so upset about? Nancy wondered. And who is he? Suddenly a feeling of dread came over her.

"You're Christy Kelley," the man blurted, adjusting his glasses. "I recognize you from TV." He paused, struggling to catch his breath. "You're not going to be able to film your story, Miss Kelley. The baby cougars have been kidnapped!"

6

A Biting Message

Nancy stared at the man, unable to believe her ears.

"The cubs are gone?" Christy asked, stunned.

"That's right," the man answered. "The kidnapper tranquilized their mother in order to take them away." Before he could explain any further, Sally Nelson appeared out of the throng of zoo visitors crowding the entrance area.

"Richard," she said, taking the man's arm. "Calm down. If we all try to think clearly, we'll have a much better chance of finding the cubs." Sally introduced herself and Richard Annenberg, the man with the ponytail, to Christy. "Richard is the director of the zoo," she explained. "And of course, Nancy and George and I are old friends." She smiled at the two girls.

"The zoo has never had anything like this happen before," Dr. Annenberg said. "And now—these cubs—without their mother around to nurse them, they will need to be bottle-fed at least every two hours. Otherwise, they won't survive." Despite Sally's plea that he relax, his voice became even more agitated.

"Richard," Sally said evenly. "I'm sure that whoever took thc cubs knows that. These cubs must be valuable to that person, and he—or she—is not going to let them die."

"I can only hope you're right," Dr. Annenberg said, seeming to grow calmer at the thought. He mopped his brow with a handkerchief. "The thief might know just how important these endangered cubs are to the zoo. But if it's ransom money he's after, he'll have to prove that the cubs are alive and well."

"I hope you won't mind if I call you Richard," Christy broke in, flashing him a syrupy smile. "This theft is a tragedy, Richard, but there's still a chance for it to end happily. In my opinion, the best way to recover the cubs is for the public to be on alert. Therefore"—she paused, looking dramatically around at the group—"the story must go on."

"Go on?" Dr. Annenberg repeated. "But what kind of story will it be without the cubs? Katie's not her usual self after being tranquilized—I don't want to disturb her."

"The taping needn't take long," Christy said

confidently. "Naturally, the story will be about the missing cubs, and Katie in the background will add an emotional element to it—a mother's plea to the public to find her missing children. Her presence will spur people on to help, even if she's been tranquilized."

Nancy stared at Christy in disbelief. How could she be so selfish? Nancy wondered. Christy obviously didn't care about poor Katie as long as she got her news story. From the look on Dr. Annenberg's face, Nancy got the impression he didn't completely buy her act, either.

After a brief pause, Christy added, "Of course, we could do the story without Katie if you really think it best. *I* happen to think that if she goes on the air, the cubs will be found much sooner."

"I see what you mean, Christy," Dr. Annenberg said. His tone was respectful but without warmth. "I'll okay the story, on one condition. If Katie seems too stressed out, we'll do it without her." He nodded, indicating the end of their conversation.

Christy opened her mouth to respond, but Dr. Annenberg had already turned to Nancy. "Are you, by any chance, *the* Nancy Drew—the detective?" he asked.

Surprised, Nancy said, "Yes, I occasionally solve mysteries."

Dr. Annenberg nodded, then seemed to hesitate for a moment. "I hope you won't mind my asking you this, but would you be interested in investigating the disappearance of the cougars?"

"But aren't the police already investigating?" Nancy asked. She felt Christy's sharp eyes boring into her.

"Yes, they left just before you arrived. Still, the more detectives, the better."

"I'd love to take on the case," Nancy said, and smiled. "I met the cubs this morning. They're adorable, and I understand their value. I'd like to do whatever I can to get them safely back with Katie." Nancy felt Christy's intense stare and shot her a quick look. Sure enough, her boss's blue eyes were riveted on her. Almost immediately, Christy dropped her gaze, but not before Nancy saw the look of annoyance in her eyes.

"Excuse me," Dr. Annenberg said in a more conversational tone. "Has anyone ever said that you two could be sisters?" He looked back and forth from Nancy to Christy. "It's uncanny how alike you look."

"*I* never would have thought so," Christy said huffily. "And I don't think many others would think so, either."

Dr. Annenberg shrugged. "Well, it was just a thought."

Nancy smiled to herself as she considered Dr. Annenberg's words. When she'd first met Christy, Nancy had been struck by the resemblance between herself and her new boss. If it hadn't been for Christy's corporate-looking clothes and makeup, the two could have been mistaken for the same person. But after getting to know Christy's personality, Nancy no longer saw the resemblance.

Glancing at Dr. Annenberg, Nancy asked, "Who discovered the theft?"

"Your cameraman—what's his name? Hawk, I think. He discovered the cubs were missing. His partner had just stopped off at my office to tell me that they had arrived and that Hawk was setting up the equipment. Suddenly, this Hawk himself rushed into my office with the news."

Nancy blinked in surprise. If Hawk was the one who'd alerted the zoo director about the missing cubs, could he have stolen them, too? He'd been alone near the nursery cage for a short time, but—

"I think we've stood here long enough," Christy snapped, abruptly derailing Nancy's train of thought. "If the zoo wants the cougars back, we'd better get on with our story now."

"Fine," Dr. Annenberg said. "I'll meet you all at Katie's cage in ten minutes. First, I promised to give Chief McGinnis at the River Heights Police Department a call and answer a few questions."

Dr. Annenberg headed back to his office, while Sally led Nancy, George, and Christy to the nursery. Once there, the WRVH crew sprang into action, setting up the rest of the equipment. Christy barked out orders, and Hawk and Joey hustled to keep up. With research notes in hand,

Nancy and George leaned against the wall, temporarily ignored by the rest of the crew.

Nancy watched as Sally went into the cage to examine Katie with a stethoscope. Katie was lying on her side, and Nancy assumed she was asleep. But at Sally's gentle touch, she raised her head lethargically, then lowered it back onto the straw.

Once she'd finished the exam, Sally went over to talk to George and Nancy. "Katie's still kind of out of it," she confided to the girls. "Whoever stole the cubs put tranquilizers in some meat and gave it to Katie. We found a small piece of hamburger meat on the floor outside the cage with part of a pill stuck inside. The medicine really zonked her, poor thing."

"She was tranquilized so she wouldn't attack the thief?" George asked.

Sally nodded. "If someone had tried to take her cubs while she wasn't tranquilized, Katie would have had their hides."

Nancy saw Richard Annenberg come in through the far front door. This time, his shirttails were neatly tucked into his trousers, and he wore a pale blue-and-white seersucker jacket and navy blue bow tie.

"We'll do a practice run-through first, then the real thing," Christy commanded. After a brief rehearsal, Hawk and Joey switched on their equipment and the camera started to roll.

Christy stood confidently in the circle of

bright light, smiling warmly at the camera. She opened her report by announcing the birth of the cubs, then quickly switched to the catnapping. She interviewed Dr. Annenberg, asking him for general information about cougars and their status as endangered creatures. Then she quizzed him about who he thought might be responsible for the deed and why.

"I questioned all zoo employees with keys to the nursery cage," Dr. Annenberg said, "and no one had left it unlocked. The culprit must have made a copy of a stolen key and then sneaked into the cage to feed the poisoned meat to Katie." He paused for a moment, then added gravely, "Whoever stole the cubs, if you're watching me now, please remember that they *must* be bottle-fed every two hours, or else they won't survive."

As Christy continued with her questions, she gestured every now and then at Katie, who lay listlessly on the nursery floor. After about five more minutes, Christy wrapped up her report, and Hawk stopped the camera. George sprang to help stow the equipment, while Nancy stayed back, keeping her eye on Christy.

"Great piece there, Christy," Joey said. "Our ratings will climb sky-high."

Instead of looking flattered at Joey's compliment, Christy frowned, putting her fingers to her lips to quiet him. Then she slipped her arm through Dr. Annenberg's and led him away, but not so far that Nancy couldn't hear every word she said.

"The theft of the cougar cubs is a terrible crime," Christy began. "As an investigative reporter, I feel compelled to find the missing cubs myself. I have the perfect skills for the task."

Nancy's jaw dropped in amazement. Why would Christy say this, after Dr. Annenberg had asked *Nancy* to investigate? Nancy exchanged glances with Dr. Annenberg, who looked completely baffled, too.

"Thank you, Richard, for all your information," Christy continued. "I promise I will not rest until I've found those cougars."

"Uh . . . I'm grateful to you for offering, Christy," Dr. Annenberg said, flustered. "But I'm sure you're busy at WRVH, and we do have others on the job." He shot a meaningful look at Nancy.

But Christy had already turned away from the zoo director and toward Hawk and Joey. "Let's get going, guys," she told them. "I want this film back at the studio pronto for editing."

Nancy tugged on George's T-shirt and nodded in the direction of the door. They slipped out into the bright sunlight.

George put on her sunglasses as Nancy told her about Christy's offer to find the missing cubs. "Christy is getting weirder and weirder," George muttered.

"I'll say," Nancy agreed. "And I have a sneaking suspicion she's going to pile on work so I won't have time to investigate the mystery myself. But why would she be acting like this?"

"As I said earlier—I'll bet she's jealous of you," George replied. "She's ambitious and wants to be a great investigative reporter. She doesn't like sharing the limelight with anyone—especially a summer intern."

Nancy shrugged. She couldn't believe that an established reporter like Christy would be jealous of her. Still, she couldn't think of any other reason for Christy's strange behavior.

Nancy gave her friend a sly smile. "I hate to do this to you, George, but would you mind telling Christy I went home sick? I want to poke around here for a while longer."

George groaned. "So I have to go back to WRVH without you for moral support?" She shook her head. "It's an unfair world."

Nancy grinned. "If I crack this case, you'll be a true hero. Thanks." Nancy gave George a thumbs-up, then headed for the infirmary to scout out Bess.

Nancy hurried along the asphalt path that wound past several cages of monkeys, all chattering as they leaped from tree to tree in their jungle habitats. She paused in front of the colobus monkeys, marveling at their furry black-and-white coats as they took turns grooming each other.

"I sure am glad *we've* got hair salons," a familiar voice said.

"Bess!" Nancy exclaimed. "Just the person I was looking for. And what are you doing with that ice-cream cone? I thought you were on a diet."

"I am." Bess's blue eyes gleamed mischievously. "The ice-cream diet. You eat it three times a day between meals—it's perfect!"

"But aren't you supposed to be working?" Nancy asked, laughing. "What would Sally say?"

Bess licked her mint chocolate chip ice cream nonchalantly. "Sally likes happy employees. She knows we work better that way."

"I can see the results," Nancy said. "Speaking of work, Dr. Annenberg has asked me to help him find the missing cougar cubs."

"Oh, I'm so glad," Bess said, her face lighting up. "The sooner we find those poor little cubs, the better. Have you found any clues yet?"

After filling Bess in on the details of her investigation, Nancy said, "I have a small task for you, Bess. Could you introduce me to Eduardo Vallejo, the cat trainer Sally mentioned? I want to talk to all the zoo employees who have keys to the cougar cage, so I'll need to meet him and also Junior Anderson, the man who takes care of the animals."

"Randy Thompson and Sally also have keys," Bess offered. "But I'm *sure* they wouldn't have stolen the cubs. For one thing, Randy's been taking a vet-school exam all day."

"And Sally was meeting with Dr. Annenberg this morning when the first attempt failed," Nancy said.

"I just saw Eduardo with the lions, near the ice-cream stand," Bess said. "Let's go and I'll introduce you."

The two girls headed for the lion habitat, where Bess pointed out Eduardo, a short man in his midtwenties with slicked-back dark hair. He stood about ten feet inside the lions' area, brandishing a whip to keep a male lion at bay. With two cracks of his whip, Eduardo signaled for the lion to retreat about ten yards, then lie down peacefully on the grass.

Taking Nancy's arm, Bess shouted out a quick introduction, which Eduardo ignored. Nancy asked him if she could question him when he was finished with the lions.

"Please! Not another word!" Eduardo commanded. "Can't you see I'm way too busy to talk? If I allow my focus to waver from this beast, I could be eaten before your very eyes."

Nancy flushed. "Sorry, sir," she said. "I'll look for you later."

Turning to Bess, Nancy murmured, "He has a point. This is definitely not the time to question him. But do you think he'll let me talk to him later?"

Bess nodded. "He's usually pretty friendly,

when he's not being a prima donna." Bess checked her watch. "It's four already. I should head back to the infirmary—Sally might be missing me."

After Bess left, Nancy wandered over to the ice-cream stand, trying to decide what to do next. She decided on ice cream. As she dug in her purse for the money, she pulled out an envelope she knew hadn't been there before. Her name was printed in block letters on the front.

Nancy paid for her ice cream and then sat down on a nearby bench. She studied the printing on the envelope before tearing it open. Inside was a note printed in the same bold block lettering:

STOP YOUR INVESTIGATION, OR I'LL TAKE A BITE OUT OF YOU.—KATIE THE COUGAR

Either this is a joke, Nancy thought grimly, or someone is trying to scare me off the case. A sudden chill ran through her as remembered the coiled snake on her car.

Just then Nancy noticed a bulge at the bottom of the envelope. She reached back inside and pulled something out.

"It's a tooth," Nancy murmured. She ran a finger over its tip, then caught her breath in surprise. A tiny pinprick of blood bubbled onto her finger.

7

Secret Sabotage

Nancy took a tissue from her purse and pressed it to her finger.

Who had put the note—and razor-sharp tooth—into her purse? she wondered. The cougar thief? And where did the tooth come from? It was much too big for a newborn cougar. Her stomach knotted. Something very creepy was going on at the zoo, and whoever sent her the note clearly meant business.

She tried to think of all the places she'd been since she and George had bought hot dogs before leaving the zoo earlier that day. That was the last time she'd looked in her purse. The note definitely hadn't been there then. It had been placed there either at the TV station or later at the zoo while Christy taped her report.

Nancy took a few bites of her ice cream, then tossed the rest into a nearby garbage can. She was feeling too upset to eat any more. Well, she decided, I'm certainly not going to be scared off the case. Maybe the thief left some clues inside the cougar habitat. First stop, Dr. Annenberg's office, to get permission to go inside, then . . . Nancy felt a surge of excitement at the thought of walking through the gate into the cougars' terrain.

Dr. Annenberg was just leaving as Nancy approached the administration building, a single-level stone structure.

"Dr. Annenberg," Nancy called out. "I'm glad I caught you." He stopped and waited for her to catch up to him. "I'd like to check out the cougar habitat," Nancy told him. "Is there a way I could safely do that?"

"I'll telephone over to the infirmary and ask Sally to meet you at Katie's cage. She'll be able to help you." The zoo director pulled a cell phone out of his pocket and punched in some numbers. After speaking into it for a moment, he hung up and told Nancy that Sally would meet her right away.

"I've already locked Prince and Katie in their cages, so it's safe for you to go in," Sally said as Nancy reached the gate. "Still, I'd like to wait here in case you need any help."

"I hate to keep you waiting, Sally," Nancy said. "I know you're busy."

"Don't worry about me. Finding the cougars is the most important thing. Plus"—Sally held up a veterinary magazine—"it'll be a good opportunity for me to catch up on some medical reading I need to do. Oh, just for your information, the habitat adjoining this one is unoccupied. We're planning to acquire some snow leopards later this summer."

"Thanks," Nancy said. She slipped through the gate and found herself in another world. Instead of the tree-shaded asphalt paths and colorful gardens of the public zoo area, the cougar habitat had coarse grass, patches of bare earth, and several piles of enormous rocks. Here and there were stands of small evergreen trees and scrubby bushes.

Nancy remembered that *cougar* and *mountain lion* were different names for the same animal, which lived in western North America and central South America. She knew that their zoo habitat had been carefully designed to resemble their natural habitats.

As she began to hunt for clues, Nancy estimated that the habitat was about three acres. Carefully, she examined the back of the building where Prince's and Katie's cages were. She found nothing unusual, noting that Katie's nursery door was padlocked shut. The thief had obviously first tried to steal the cubs earlier that morning, Nancy mused, which was why the cub had ended up outside the cage with the door ajar. Had Katie scared the thief away?

Nancy knew that if she could pinpoint a motive for the catnapping, she would be a lot closer to identifying the culprit. She mused for what felt like the hundredth time: were the cubs taken for ransom money? For the black market Sally had mentioned? Or for some other, more mysterious reason?

Finding nothing near the building, Nancy continued her search, moving over to a grove of small hemlock trees about thirty feet from the cougar cages. She scanned the shaded area underneath the low-hanging branches, poking in the thin bed of evergreen needles with the toe of her sandal. Then she walked over to one of the mountains of rocks and checked its crevices and nooks.

At the base of the rocks on the far side, Nancy saw a glimmer of something reflecting the sunlight. She bent down and picked up a pair of mirrored sunglasses that had been wedged between a crack in the rocks. Nancy studied them carefully, hoping they might be a clue to the case.

A thin piece of masking tape was stuck on the inside rim of the glasses. Something was written on it, perhaps a name, but the writing was smudged to the point of being illegible. The only letter Nancy could read was a capital *V*. Frowning, Nancy rubbed the smudged part, which smeared her fingertip. Black marker, she decided.

Nancy dropped the sunglasses into her purse and continued to explore the habitat. At the far end was an eight-foot-high stone wall—the wall that encircled the zoo, she guessed.

Jogging over to it, Nancy spotted a padlocked iron gate in the wall. Nancy peered through the gate's bars and saw a sidewalk bordering a quiet street. Across the street was a row of shabby Victorian houses.

Squinting, Nancy made out a street sign on a lamppost about fifty feet to her right: Oak Street. Someone with a key to the gate could have sneaked the cougars through it and then driven them away, Nancy reasoned.

Nancy strolled around the rest of the habitat but didn't find anything else. Finally, she returned to the front gate, where Sally was waiting to let her out.

"Look what I found," Nancy said. Handing Sally the sunglasses, she explained where she had picked them up. Then she pointed to the smudged name and the *V*.

As Sally studied the glasses, her eyes clouded over. Is it my imagination, Nancy thought, or is Sally upset by something?

Sally sighed. "Eduardo Vallejo has a pair of sunglasses exactly like these."

Nancy perked up. *V* for *Vallejo.*

"But Eduardo often goes inside the habitat,"

Sally went on, handing the glasses back to Nancy. "These glasses prove nothing. He could have lost them months ago."

These glasses may not prove that Eduardo is the culprit, Nancy mused, but they don't disprove it, either.

"Is Eduardo likely to wander around the habitat?" Nancy asked. "Would he have gone behind those rocks for any reason?"

"You never know with Eduardo," Sally answered uncertainly. "But if these are his glasses, I'm sure he had good reasons for being in that particular spot."

Like waiting for the perfect opportunity to steal four newborn cougar cubs? Nancy thought. Nancy couldn't guess what Eduardo's motive for theft might be, but he had the keys to Katie's cage; he was trained in handling wild cats and he had dropped his glasses in a perfect hiding spot for a thief to wait and watch for his chance. Eduardo had definitely joined Hawk at the top of Nancy's list of suspects.

Nancy thanked Sally for her help, then set off for Dr. Annenberg's office to see if he could help her track down Eduardo. As she rounded a curve in the path that ran along the tiger habitat, she heard leaves rustling ahead of her. A bright purple blur shimmered through gaps in the shrubbery. Was someone hiding in the bushes? she wondered with a sudden prickle of fear.

Just then the purple shimmer emerged from

the bushes. It was a metallic purple shirt worn by Eduardo Vallejo atop tight black pants. Nancy stopped in surprise.

"Hello," Eduardo said. "You're Bess's friend, right?" Nancy nodded. "I suppose you're wondering what I was doing in the bushes. Here, come look."

Eduardo moved aside some branches on the nearest bush. Nancy hesitantly stood on her tiptoes to look down toward the ground through the opening he'd made. About five feet away—though it seemed like inches to Nancy—stood a gorgeous orange tiger with black stripes. Nancy reached out to touch the fence that separated them for assurance. The tiger stood perfectly still, his ears pricked forward, his eyes gazing at her.

"Isn't he a beauty?" Eduardo said. "I couldn't resist sneaking a peek at him when he wasn't aware of me. But of course I made too much noise and disturbed him stalking a bird."

"He *is* an amazing-looking creature," Nancy agreed, admiring the tiger's statuelike calm. "Thank you for showing him to me." Settling back down on her feet, Nancy turned toward Eduardo. "I'm glad I ran into you. I was actually on my way to find you."

Eduardo frowned, his thick black brows forming a single line. "Why?" he asked suspiciously.

"I wanted to ask you a few questions."

Eduardo let out a low growl. Not unlike one of

his wild cats, Nancy thought. "It won't take long, I promise," Nancy assured him.

"I answer to no one!" Eduardo snapped. *"You*, a teenager, want to question, *me*, an experienced trainer of wild cats, about—I'm guessing—the missing cougar cubs. Well, I will not have it! I know nothing about the theft, and I will not allow myself to be insulted by your questions."

This guy has a major ego problem, Nancy thought, taking a step back. And why is he so sure I want to ask him about the cubs? It's almost as if he's feeling guilty about them.

"Forget the questions," Nancy said soothingly. She took the sunglasses from her pocket and held them out to him. "Here, I thought you might want your glasses back."

Eduardo wrinkled his brow. Then he reached into his pocket and whipped out an identical pair of sunglasses. "But I haven't lost my glasses," he said.

Nancy blinked. "That's funny," she said. She took another look at the glasses in her hand. "These were found in the cougar habitat. They have the initial *V* on the inside. Sally thought they were yours."

"Let me see." Eduardo took the glasses and studied the tape on the inside. Then he compared the two pairs of glasses in his hands. "I don't know who these belong to," he said, handing the lost ones back to Nancy. "I cannot help you. And in case you're interested, I have not been inside the cougar habitat all day."

"I wonder who these belong to, then?" Nancy said, half to herself.

"I said I don't know," Eduardo said stiffly. "There are other people with the letter *V* in their names, you know."

"Sally mentioned that you used to be a lion trainer in the circus," Nancy said, hoping he'd loosen up and talk about his background. That must be where he got his notion of fashion, she thought, but she said, "That sounds like an interesting job."

"Dangerous, exciting, thrilling, yes," Eduardo said with a sweep of his hand. "I don't know about 'interesting.'"

"Why did you leave it?" Nancy asked.

Eduardo scowled. "I thought I said no questions." He paused, looking at Nancy appraisingly. "If you were using those sunglasses as a ploy to get me to talk—" He leaned forward, his dark eyes bulging with anger. "I'm telling you one more time, and that's it: mind your own business!"

Nancy took a step backward as Eduardo shook his fist at her. Then he brushed by her and stormed down the path.

That guy's definitely worth investigating further, Nancy concluded.

Nancy set off in the opposite direction from Eduardo. Now what? she wondered. Around a bend in the path, she caught sight of Bess talking to a tall, auburn-haired young man outside the infirmary door.

"Nancy," Bess called out excitedly, waving her over. "I want you to meet Randy Thompson, the assistant vet here. Randy, this is my best friend, Nancy Drew."

"Hello, Nancy," Randy said, extending his hand. A smile lit up his handsome face as he greeted her. "I missed all the action here this morning. I was taking a school exam."

As Nancy chatted with Randy, she noticed Bess glancing at him shyly out of the corner of her eye. "I'll let you guys get back to your conversation," Nancy told them, smiling. "I've got to go."

"That's too bad," Randy said. "I was about to suggest taking a monorail ride."

"We'd love to," Bess piped up.

Just then Sally came out of the infirmary and beckoned to Randy. "I need your help, Randy. The flamingo I brought in this morning needs its wing set."

"Sure, Sally—no problem," Randy replied.

Bess looked crestfallen as Randy followed Sally into the infirmary. At the door, however, Randy stopped and said, "You girls should take the ride without me. It's a great way to see the animals, and at this time of day, it's not crowded."

Nancy looked at her watch. "Five o'clock, Bess. Time for you to stop working, anyway. Why don't we take a spin on the monorail? I'd like to get a look at the whole zoo. Maybe I'll get some ideas about this case."

Bess still looked disappointed, but she agreed. Ten minutes later the two girls were sitting in the last car of the monorail as it rumbled along the track eight feet above the ground.

"Randy didn't exaggerate when he said it's not crowded at this time," Nancy commented. They were the only people on board besides the driver.

The driver described the animals they passed on a loudspeaker. The monorail crossed through habitats of several species of birds and giraffes. It skirted the habitats of the rhinoceroses and bears, moving along just outside the chain-link fence. Nancy looked at each habitat carefully but didn't see anything that helped her investigation.

"Hey, check out those hyenas!" Bess exclaimed. "They look pretty fierce."

The monorail track skimmed the crest of a grassy hill next to the hyena habitat. Nancy peered below at the skinny doglike creatures with brown fur. Their eyes glinted menacingly as the monorail glided by.

Suddenly, the monorail jolted. Nancy's stomach lurched as their car lost its mooring and swung off the track. Bess screamed. Nancy ducked her head, bracing herself as the monorail tumbled down the small hill and crashed against the chain-link fence.

8

Dining with Danger

Nancy looked up to see a hyena running full speed straight toward her. It threw itself hard against the fence that stood between the mangled monorail car and the habitat. The fence bulged with the beast's impact as it lunged again, baring its sharp teeth.

"Nan!" Bess shrieked, gripping her friend's arm. "The fence is going to give way!"

Nancy stiffened, expecting to feel the sharp teeth of the wild animal tearing into her at any second.

A second hyena rushed the fence. All Nancy could see was its enormous mouth flashing huge, deadly-looking fangs. That fence won't hold, Nancy thought in terror. We're done for unless we do something.

She and Bess cowered as the creature made another attempt at them, making a chattering noise.

"Unhook your seat belt, Bess," Nancy urged as she struggled to unbuckle hers. "We have to get out of here fast."

The monorail driver ran up. "Are you girls all right?" he asked anxiously. "You didn't hurt your heads, did you?" He helped Nancy and Bess undo their seat belts, then pulled them out of the car.

"No." Nancy eyed the hyenas nervously. "We didn't get hurt from the crash, but those hyenas look pretty hungry."

"Don't worry about the fence. It'll hold. It's stronger than it looks."

Despite the driver's reassuring words, he cast an uneasy glance at the hyenas as he helped Nancy and Bess climb up the hill to the monorail track.

"What happened?" Nancy asked when they'd reached the top. The hyenas had stopped charging the fence and were pacing together, growling and baring their heinous teeth.

"I don't know," the driver replied. Now that they seemed out of danger, Nancy noticed the man's voice was shaking. "We were going along when I felt this bump along the track. The next thing I knew, the train had derailed and we were falling down the hill. I'm glad it's the end of the day and there were no other passengers." He stared at the five-car monorail lying in a jumble at the bottom of the hill. His hand trembled as he took a radio handset from his pocket and punched in a number.

Was it a freak accident, or something more ominous? Nancy wondered as she walked slowly along the track, studying it for flaws. The single steel rail gleamed in the late-afternoon light, and Nancy averted her eyes from the glare. As she shifted her gaze, she noticed a battered metal bar about four feet long lying across the track. She stooped to pick it up, but it was too heavy. Her heart skipped a beat. This must be what knocked the train off the track, she concluded. Had someone put it there on purpose?

Nancy looked around. They were in a far corner of the zoo. There were no pedestrian paths in sight—just the monorail track and the hyena habitat backed up against the zoo's outer wall. Someone could have easily climbed over the wall from the street and placed the bar on the track without being seen, she realized.

Nancy called the driver over and showed him the metal bar.

"I have no idea what that thing is," he said, kicking it with his boot. "It wasn't there on my previous go-round. I just tried to call Security, but my radio's not working. I'd better get a good look at that train so I can report its condition to

Dr. Annenberg. Can you girls hold on a bit? I know you must be shaken." He didn't wait for an answer but began easing himself down the hill to inspect the front car of the train.

"Let's get out of here, Nancy," Bess whined. "It's been a long, lousy day. And I could use a shower."

Nancy looked at Bess's dirt-smeared face. Her white tank top had grass stains on it, and her miniskirt was torn at the hem. "I'm sure I could use one, too," Nancy said. She held out her hands, caked with dirt from the fall. "But we'd better wait until the driver gets back."

"What an awful accident," Bess declared.

"If it was an accident," Nancy whispered.

"You mean you think someone put that bar across the track on purpose?" Bess asked.

Nancy shrugged. "How else could it have gotten there?" She paused. "Not only that, Bess, but I think someone saw us get on the monorail and then put it there."

"Oh, Nancy, we've *got* to solve this case," Bess said worriedly. "The cubs aren't the only ones in danger."

"I know," Nancy said solemnly. "But I'm convinced that I've already come across some important evidence. Otherwise, someone wouldn't be so desperate to stop us."

Nancy felt a knot tighten in her stomach as she thought of the recent scary incidents at the zoo: the cobra, the animal tooth, and now the monorail accident. Bess is right, she thought grimly. We are in danger.

Once the driver had finished his inspection, he said, "I'll lead you back to the monorail station. I have to track down Dr. Annenberg. He'll probably want to talk to the two of you."

The driver led Nancy and Bess back to the monorail station, the one Nancy had first noticed near the zoo entrance. It was now six o'clock, and the zoo had closed half an hour earlier, but the guard at the front gate was still letting out a few stragglers.

Nancy and Bess thanked the monorail driver, who was on his way to tell Dr. Annenberg the news, before they hurried through the exit.

As Nancy and Bess drove away in Bess's car, Nancy glanced at her watch. "Oh, no," she said in a frustrated tone of voice. "I wanted to watch Christy's story on the evening news, but it's too late now."

When they reached the WRVH parking lot, Nancy thanked Bess for the ride and hopped into her Mustang.

At home Nancy yelled hello to Hannah, the housekeeper, and, without waiting for a reply, ran upstairs to take a quick shower.

After dressing in a purple T-shirt, a denim skirt, and some comfortable sandals, she hurried down to the kitchen.

"Hannah?" Nancy called out. There was no answer. A note lay on the kitchen counter: Hannah had gone to visit a sick friend; Nancy's father would not be home for dinner; there was a phone message from George: pick up Bess and meet Hawk, Joey, and her at Zamboni's Pizza.

Great, thought Nancy. She'd have a chance to talk to both Hawk and Joey—and be able to take them off her suspect list, she hoped.

"A shower and a change of clothes sure can work wonders," Bess said, smoothing her pale pink sundress over her lap as they rode along in Nancy's car. "Though every time I think of those hyenas, I get the creeps."

"Ditto," Nancy said. "Think pizza instead."

"Nice try, Nan," Bess replied. "But when I get the hyenas out of my head, all I can see are those cute cubs. Have you figured out how Hawk lost his ring inside Katie's cage?"

Nancy shook her head. "I want to ask him about it tonight. I think either he must have stolen a key or he has an accomplice with one."

The pizzeria was on a busy intersection not far from the zoo. A flashing neon sign in the window announced its name: Zamboni's.

Zamboni as in Joey Zamboni? Nancy wondered.

"Nancy, Bess!" George called out as they entered. "Over here." She was seated at a large round table in the middle of the restaurant. George sat between Joey and Hawk, and before

Nancy could signal Bess to sit next to Joey, she had taken the chair next to Hawk.

Nancy had wanted to talk to Hawk first, but she sat down next to Joey with a smile.

"I thought you were sick," Joey said to Nancy. "Are you sure you're up for pizza?"

"I'm feeling much better," Nancy said, exchanging a quick glance with George. "And I'm sure a slice of pizza will cure me completely."

"It will?" Hawk said doubtfully. "Well, I suppose Joey's dad's homemade pizzas *could* cure just about anything. Here comes our pie. I hope you like yours with peppers and extra cheese."

As they all dug into the pizza, Nancy turned to Joey. In a lowered voice, she started right in with her questions. "Joey, remember the end of the B-roll? I'm wondering if the shadow on the tape could have been the thief. Don't you think we should tell Sally or Dr. Annenberg about it?"

Joey abruptly dropped his gaze. "I doubt that shadow was any big deal, Nancy," he said in a hushed voice.

"You never know," Nancy pressed. "The smallest clue might be the one that leads us to the cubs. And anyway, what's the down side of showing Dr. Annenberg the tape?"

Joey sucked in his breath, eyeing Nancy nervously. "Promise you'll back off if I tell you what happened at the shoot?" he said. "It doesn't have anything to do with the theft."

Nancy nodded. "It's a deal, so long as you tell me every detail you can think of." Nancy knew that regardless of what Joey said, the shadow could be *very* important.

Joey rolled his eyes, then reluctantly said, "When the shoot ended, Hawk went off to get a soda while I was supposed to be packing up our stuff. But just for fun—well, I decided to shoot a scene myself. You see, I'm getting sick of being just a soundman. I've always wanted to get behind a camera."

"So *you* shot the scene with the shadow at the door?" Nancy asked just to be sure.

"I didn't see the shadow while I was filming, though," Joey said. "Only afterward."

"When did you next see Hawk?" Nancy asked.

"About ten minutes after I left Katie's cage, back at the van." Joey gave Nancy a pleading look. "Don't tell anyone about this, okay? I could get in big trouble."

So Joey's worried about getting *himself* in trouble, Nancy mused. But he doesn't realize he's implicating Hawk.

Nancy assured him she'd keep his secret. She picked up a second piece of pizza and started nibbling. She could feel her excitement mounting as she realized that Hawk could definitely have cast the shadow at the door.

As the crew started to think about dessert, Nancy signaled Bess to follow her to the ladies' room. On their way, she asked Bess to switch places with her during dessert so she could question Hawk.

When they returned to the table, Nancy took Bess's seat.

"We have the best sundaes in River Heights," Joey bragged. "Homemade ice cream with toppings my mother makes herself."

That settled the question of dessert.

After the sundaes were served, Nancy turned to Hawk. "I missed Christy's story on Katie and the cubs. How did it go?"

Hawk scowled. "It went okay, I guess, but I wouldn't be the best judge. It bugs me that we did that story at all."

"Why? Do you think it was hard on Katie?"

"It's not that," Hawk said bitterly. "It's just that I hate zoos. I can't stand seeing all those animals cooped up in cages. They'd be much better off in the wild where they belong."

"But many of them are endangered species," Nancy responded. "They're actually being protected at the zoo."

"Yeah, right." Hawk snorted. "How would you like to be taken away from your home and stuck in a cage? No Mustang, no summer internship, no freedom."

"But what about the cubs, Hawk?" Nancy said. "They will ensure that the species survives, and someday the zoos will be able to repopulate the wild with cougars."

Hawk threw his spoon into his sundae. "I'm

not talking about pie-in-the-sky future. I am talking about now. What about *these* cubs? What about Katie? Don't *they* deserve to be free?"

Nancy was taken aback at the emotion behind Hawk's words. I've certainly hit a sore spot, she thought.

Hawk wasn't finished. "They'll spend the rest of their lives caged up. And what do we do about it? We put them on television so everyone will come see them and the zoo will make more money to get more animals to put behind bars."

"But Christy's story might help reunite them with their mother," Nancy suggested.

"If Katie and the cubs hadn't been in the zoo in the first place, none of this would have happened." Hawk's dark eyes glittered fiercely.

"But they *are* in this predicament. Shouldn't we try—" Nancy began.

Hawk flew out of his chair in rage and lunged toward Nancy.

9

Over the Wall

Hawk stopped short, his face inches away from Nancy's.

"I repeat: How would you like to live your life in a cage?" he yelled.

The restaurant fell silent as all the customers turned to stare at Hawk.

Nancy, too, was shocked into silence by his anger.

Joey stood and walked over to Hawk. "Hey," he said in a calm voice, "why don't we just sit down and finish the sundaes?" He picked up Hawk's chair and held it for him. "My dad's watching from the kitchen," Joey added with a smile. "You don't want to get me in trouble with the old man."

Hawk sat down and the fury seemed to drain away. No one spoke.

"I'm sorry, Nancy, everybody," Hawk said. "Let's drop the subject. Just thinking about zoos gets me riled."

"Hawk," Joey said quietly, "I think you owe them an explanation as well."

Hawk gave Joey a long, searching look, which Joey returned. By the time Hawk broke eye contact, he'd obviously made a decision.

"Okay," Hawk said. "It's not something I put on my résumé, so I'd appreciate it if you didn't spread it around the office." He looked at Nancy and George, who nodded mutely.

"When I was a kid, I did something really stupid and got caught. I took my dad's car for a joyride, only I didn't have a license and it was his brand-new Mercedes. Typical stuff for a typical kid. But I didn't have a typical dad. Car hit tree. Kid winds up in jail." Hawk let out half a laugh. "My dad knew everyone in the town I grew up in. He made a deal with the sheriff to let me sit there for three days before coming to get me."

"Hawk," George said, "your dad's the one who should be in jail."

"Well, that was about the only time he ever lost his cool. He told my mom I'd gone camping. When she found out, boy, my dad lived to regret it." Hawk laughed again.

Joey jumped in, grinning broadly. "Yeah. Tell them what you got for your sixteenth birthday."

Hawk's last bit of tension seemed to slip away. Laughing, he said, "Mom made him buy *me* a brand-new Mercedes. It was three weeks after I'd gotten my driver's license."

"You're kidding!" Bess exclaimed.

"But you don't drive a Mercedes," Nancy pointed out.

"Nope," Hawk said. "I don't go in for that stuff. Life and freedom is more my line. I sold it to pay for film school."

"So it all turned out okay—with your folks, I mean," George asked.

"Yeah," Hawk said. "We're cool."

Nancy sat back and took a sip of soda. Cool, except on the subject of cages, she thought. Obviously, Hawk's three days in jail had left him with strong feelings about cages—and zoos. She had no doubt in her mind that he could have taken the little cougars just to get them out of the zoo. But what would he have done with them? She wanted to ask him about the shadow at the end of the B-roll, but she didn't dare provoke him again.

"That was a great dinner, guys," Hawk said, breaking into Nancy's thoughts. "How about a movie? My treat, to make up for putting you all through that little display."

Joey brightened. "I'm game. Anyone else?"

George agreed, but Bess stifled a yawn. "Count me out," she said. "Sleep calls."

Nancy thought fast. "I'll drive you home, Bess," she offered. "I'm tired, too."

After paying her share of the bill, Nancy slipped away to look up Hawk's address in a phone booth near the restaurant door. Then she and Bess said goodbye to their friends and headed out the door to the Mustang.

As Nancy drove down the street, she told Bess what she was thinking. "That was a good story Hawk told, and it may be true, but that much emotion makes me think he could definitely be our culprit."

"I never heard anyone get so upset about zoos," Bess said. "I never even thought of them that way."

"Hawk is a guy who takes things seriously," Nancy said.

"I'll say," Bess replied. "For a moment I thought he was going to strangle you."

Nancy laughed. "You and me both." At the corner, she turned the car onto the street that passed by the zoo entrance.

"Hey, this isn't the way to my house," Bess said.

"No, it's the way to Hawk's place," Nancy explained. "I just thought you might like to drop by there with me while he's at the movies. We'll just have a look around for clues."

"Or even the cubs," Bess added. "I'm game."

But Nancy wasn't listening to Bess. She was staring at the zoo entrance up ahead. "Look,

Bess!" she cried. "Someone's climbing over the wall!"

Sure enough, a ladder was propped against the zoo wall beside the locked entrance. A blond woman in white slacks straddled the top of the wall. Swinging a slim leg over it, the woman paused for a moment, then jumped, disappearing into the zoo.

Nancy slammed on her brakes. "That's Christy Kelley!" she exclaimed.

"Christy Kelley, as in your boss?" Bess asked, amazed. "But what's she doing here?"

"I don't know, Bess. Let's go find out."

Nancy parked the car half a block from the zoo entrance, about fifty feet behind Christy's red sedan. Dangling from the luggage rack on Christy's car were several pieces of rope. Christy must have tied the ladder onto her car, Nancy guessed. Had Christy sneaked into the zoo so that she could start her own investigation of the stolen cubs?

After scrambling out of the Mustang, Nancy and Bess dashed for the ladder. Nancy made sure it was secure against the wall, then she and Bess quickly climbed it. Sitting on top, they looked down at a grassy area that would make a soft landing for them.

"How will we get back out once we're in?" Bess asked anxiously, studying the eight-foot wall.

"Let's worry about that later," Nancy said.

"Come on." By the light of the full moon, Nancy caught a glimpse of Christy hurrying down the asphalt path that led to the zoo administration offices.

First she, then Bess took the plunge and landed with two quiet thuds. They took off after Christy. As they rounded a corner, Nancy was glad to see a lamp glowing from the window of Dr. Annenberg's office. If he's still at the zoo, she thought, he'll be able to let us out the gate.

Past the administration building, the path forked three ways. Christy's light-colored shirt was barely visible as she took the middle path. Nancy and Bess kept her in sight until she rounded a corner by the elephant habitat.

Bess came to a dead stop and moaned. "Don't walk so fast, Nan. When I chose these shoes tonight, I wasn't expecting a forced march." Nancy glanced at Bess's high heels, then at the path ahead. On the right, two enormous hulking forms—elephants, Nancy guessed—swayed ever so slightly as they dozed. To the left was a dark, shedlike building—some sort of exhibit house, Nancy concluded. But where had Christy gone?

"We've lost her," Nancy whispered.

"Keep going," Bess said, rubbing her heel. "My foot feels better, and Christy's probably up ahead."

"Okay, Bess, let's hur—" A force like a load of bricks hit Nancy in the back. She stumbled forward as Bess crumpled onto the ground next to her. Stunned, Nancy gasped for air. She felt powerful arms grab her around the waist and haul her forward. Still struggling for breath, she tried to identify her assailant, but it was too dark. All she could see was someone's legs clad in a pair of black jeans, and Bess's body being dragged on the other side of them.

The person came to a stop near the shed. A door opened, and within seconds, Nancy was thrown inside. She felt Bess land on top of her, and then the door banged shut. Its lock clicked ominously.

A strange, swift, fluttering noise rose up in the pitch-dark room. Nancy heard a high-pitched squeak, and then another. She cast her eyes from side to side, frantically searching for the slightest hint of light. But it was as dark as pitch. A bat flew by their heads, and Bess let out a piercing scream.

10

Bat Attack

Nancy froze as she realized where they were—trapped inside the bat house!

"Bess, stay down!" Nancy shouted as the creatures flitted around them.

"Ugh," Bess grunted. She rolled away from where she had landed on top of Nancy, then crouched next to her.

Nancy could hear the constant rustling whisper of bat wings.

"Help, Nancy! There's a bat coming at me!" Bess screamed.

Bess ducked down, hiding her head in her arms. The bat's soft, furry body flew past, brushing Nancy's hand. Nancy shuddered, wondering how she and Bess would be able to escape from the bat house.

Slowly, Nancy's eyes adjusted to the darkness. A sliver of moonlight crept in through a tiny window near the roof, and Nancy could just discern the outline of the door behind her. Running her hand over it, she felt a knob with a tiny hole in the center. Suddenly, she had an idea.

"Bess, give me your barrette," she commanded.

Bess handed her barrette to Nancy, and Nancy went to work on the door. After several seconds of poking around, Nancy felt the lock spring open. "We're free!" she exclaimed in relief, opening the door a crack.

Peeking through it, Nancy saw no one directly outside. "The coast is clear," she whispered, opening the door wider. She and Bess hurried out, along with a few escaping bats.

After shutting the door, Nancy paused for a moment to catch her breath. "I wonder who locked us in there," she whispered uneasily, scanning the darkness for signs of their attacker.

"Someone in black jeans," Bess said. "It couldn't have been Christy. She's wearing white slacks."

A soft murmur filled the air. What's that? Nancy wondered, listening. Bats—or humans?

Nancy and Bess crept silently down the path by the elephant habitat. About fifty feet away, close to where the three paths joined by the administration building, Nancy saw two figures huddled together. Clouds had obscured the moonlight, so she couldn't make out who they were. She could see that they were talking, but she couldn't hear what they were saying.

A moment later the clouds passed and Nancy instantly recognized the two people. "It's Christy and Eduardo," she said, grabbing Bess by the arm.

Bess gasped. "Is he wearing black jeans?"

"I can't see. Let's sneak closer."

But as Nancy and Bess stepped forward, Christy and Eduardo moved apart, melting into the darkness. By the time Nancy and Bess arrived at the juncture of the three paths, the two of them were nowhere to be seen.

"Where'd they go?" Nancy mumbled in frustration. She gazed down the other two paths, which stretched into black shadowy voids. She took a step forward.

"Don't even think about it, Nancy," Bess said, with a determined shake of her head. "We're not going on another wild-goose chase. We're going home." Without waiting for Nancy's answer, Bess turned and limped toward the zoo offices.

By the moonlight Nancy saw that her watch read eleven o'clock. "You're right, Bess," Nancy said, catching up. "Time to go home."

Just as she spoke, the lights went out in Dr. Annenberg's office, and Nancy recognized the zoo director's tall form in the doorway. "Dr. Annenberg," Nancy said, greeting him. "I'm so glad to see you. Bess and I were tracking down some clues here tonight when someone shut us in the bat house."

Dr. Annenberg looked shocked. "That's awful. How did you girls get out?"

Nancy told Dr. Annenberg about the attack and admitted to her own skill at picking locks.

"I'm going to have to report this to the police," Dr. Annenberg said gravely. Then he yawned and rubbed his eyes. "I've just spent the evening poring through old employee files, looking for clues as to who might have taken the cubs, and why."

"Did you have any luck?" Bess asked.

Dr. Annenberg shook his head. "I'm completely stumped. I can't find anything in any employee's background that would suggest a motive for taking those cubs. No one is in obvious need of money, and we haven't received a ransom note."

Nancy gave Dr. Annenberg a sketchy summary of the case so far, from her point of view. But she didn't tell him about seeing Christy sneaking into the zoo tonight. The last thing she needed was more trouble with Christy. She also kept her suspicions about Eduardo to herself. She didn't want Dr. Annenberg to act differently toward Eduardo the next day. If Eduardo *was* the thief and he felt his boss suspected him, he might panic and disappear with the cubs.

After Nancy had finished updating Dr. Annenberg, he escorted her and Bess back to the zoo entrance and unlocked the gate. They all filed through it, and then Dr. Annenberg locked it again. Before strolling off to the employee parking lot, he said, "Thank you for all your hard work on the case so far, Nancy. I didn't expect you to put in such late hours when I asked you to help with it."

Nancy smiled at Dr. Annenberg. "You're welcome," she said. "I'm sure we'll figure out what's going on soon."

They said good night, then Nancy scanned the area around the gate. Christy's ladder and car were gone. For all their trouble, Nancy was no wiser as to what Christy had been doing there.

The following day, Friday, dawned clear and hot. After sleeping later than usual, Nancy arrived at the WRVH offices shortly before eleven o'clock. Her sleeveless black cotton dress felt clingy, and her forehead was damp with perspiration.

"You're late," George teased. "See all the work you stuck me with?" She swept her hand over their empty desks.

Nancy laughed, then said in a hushed voice, "Christy's been way too busy to *think* about us interns, much less give us work." She glanced around the room. Four reporters sat at desks up front. Otherwise, the room was empty.

"Wait till you hear this, George," Nancy whispered. She proceeded to tell George about seeing Christy at the zoo. By the time Nancy had finished, George was staring at her open-mouthed.

"But what was Christy doing there so late at night?" George asked.

Nancy shrugged. "Maybe she was investigating the case of the missing cubs, just as she promised."

"Maybe," George said. "I wonder how she got back over the wall. She doesn't strike me as the rock-climbing type."

"Your guess is as good as mine."

"So what's next?" George asked.

"I'd like to review the B-roll again for any clues I might have missed," Nancy replied as she gathered up a pad of paper and a pen. "You stay here and keep an eye on things. I'll be back in a little while."

"No hurry, Nancy," George said. "I haven't seen Christy all morning. You'll be able to look at the B-roll for as long as you like."

Nancy gave George a thumbs-up, then went in search of Linda Wong to ask if she could see the B-roll again.

"Sure thing, Nancy," Linda said cheerfully.

She opened a file drawer in her editing room and scanned the alphabetized tapes. "Hmm. The zoo B-roll isn't here. Let me check one other place." Linda hunted around some shelves, then turned to Nancy with a puzzled look. "That's strange. It's missing. Maybe Christy reviewed it yesterday and took it back to her office for some reason."

Nancy had an uneasy suspicion that the B-roll wasn't misplaced. Someone had stolen it—perhaps Christy Kelley.

Nancy thanked Linda and went in search of Christy. Along the way, she ran into Hawk and Joey.

"Have you guys seen the tape of the B-roll from the cougar shoot yesterday?" she asked, carefully watching Hawk's face. "Linda can't find it.

"It must be misfiled, then," Hawk said with a shrug. "They often are." Joey just shook his head, and the two guys continued on their way.

Hawk *seemed* unconcerned about the tape, Nancy mused, but she couldn't be totally sure.

As Nancy approached Christy's office, she heard several quick steps behind her. Turning, Nancy quickly stepped out of the way as Christy came running down the hall toward her office, her over-the-shoulder purse banging against her side. Her normally neat blond hair was a mess, and her face wore an anxious, harried look.

"I hope you don't need me right now, Nancy," Christy said, squeezing past her in the doorway.

Christy plopped her purse down on her desk, then turned her back on Nancy and picked up the phone.

"Christy, I do need you," Nancy said, "but I'll be quick."

Christy hung up the phone, then whirled around and glared at Nancy. "Better be. I've been out all morning, and I plan to be out most of the afternoon, at least until three-thirty, and I've got a pile of work to do now."

Undeterred by Christy's manner, Nancy asked her if she had the missing B-roll.

"Huh-uh," Christy said, shaking her head no. "I haven't seen it since yesterday. It's not in Linda's editing room?"

"Linda can't find it anywhere." Nancy studied Christy's bland expression. Maybe Christy was telling the truth. Maybe someone else had taken the film.

"By the way, Christy," Nancy continued, not taking her eyes off her boss. "Were you at the zoo last night? I was there to meet my friend Bess, who had to work late, and I thought I saw you."

"What?" Christy snapped, her face like a thundercloud. "You must be mistaken. I was certainly not there." She drew herself up indignantly, then stormed toward her office door. "Are you quite finished with your questions, Nancy? You'll make me late for my lunch date." Without waiting for a response, Christy marched past Nancy toward an open elevator door.

After the door slid shut, Nancy turned back toward Christy's office. It was the perfect opportunity to search it—for the B-roll or for any other clue that might link Christy to the missing cubs.

Nancy ran to find George, who agreed to be the lookout while Nancy searched the office.

"What are friends for, anyway," George said, "if not to provide watchdog service from time to time?"

They stopped at Christy's door, and Nancy took a look around. The coast was clear. George took up her post outside as Nancy entered and closed the door behind her.

Christy's office was spare and meticulously neat, with only a desk, a file cabinet, and a bookshelf worth exploring. Nancy made a beeline for Christy's desk. On top was her purse.

Uh-oh, Nancy thought. I hope Christy isn't coming right back for it.

Hurrying, Nancy opened the top drawer of the desk. Inside were pads of paper, Post-its, and computer disks, all neatly arranged. No luck here, Nancy thought glumly. She closed the drawer and opened the next one.

A red cashmere cardigan lay folded inside. Nancy lifted it, and a stab of excitement ran through her. Directly underneath the sweater was a white cardboard case labeled "Zoo B-roll." So Christy had the B-roll after all! Nancy thought. Why did she lie?

Nancy reached out to take the case when she heard Christy's voice outside the door. "Hold the elevator, please," Christy yelled. "I just have to grab my purse."

Before Nancy could react, the doorknob turned.

11

A Wild Accusation

"Christy!" George's words rang out from outside the door. "There's a surprise for you in the newsroom."

"A what?" Christy said, sounding uncertain. Nancy held her breath as she watched the doorknob. Suddenly, it stopped turning. "It's not my birthday or anything," Christy went on.

"Come on—I'll show you," George said. Then the two voices trailed away down the hall.

Nancy grinned in relief. Way to go, George, she thought. When she could no longer hear Christy's footsteps, Nancy sprang into action. She knew it would be only a moment until Christy returned, and she hated to think what Christy would do if she discovered the reason for George's ruse.

Her fingers shaking, Nancy removed the B-roll from the drawer and slipped it into a manila file folder. Then she carefully smoothed Christy's sweater back into place. After closing the drawer, Nancy tiptoed to the office door and peeked outside.

"Nancy!" a voice said. "I was expecting to see Christy, not you." Surprised, Nancy stepped back as Hawk's face appeared in the doorway, inches away from hers.

What was Hawk doing there? Nancy wondered. Was he looking for Christy, or was he trying to eavesdrop?

"Excuse me, Hawk," Nancy said as she slipped by him into the corridor. Closing Christy's door behind her, she looked him in the eye. "Are you busy right now? I have some questions about the B-roll you guys shot at the zoo."

Hawk shot her a puzzled look. "Questions? Well, I guess I have a minute. What is it you want to know?"

Nancy glanced down the hall. Christy and George were nowhere to be seen, but Nancy didn't want to stick around.

"Can we go into an empty editing room, Hawk?" Nancy asked. "I'd like to sit down."

With a weary sigh, Hawk sat down on a chair in one of the editing rooms, and Nancy sat next to him. "I'm tired," Hawk confessed. "The movie went on forever last night. You're lucky you opted out of going."

George could verify whether Hawk was really at the movie and therefore not at the zoo with Christy last night. Still, Nancy thought, Hawk and Christy *could* be allies in the cougarnapping scheme—if one of them had stolen a key to Katie's cage.

"So, what's your question about the B-roll?" Hawk asked.

Gathering her thoughts, Nancy asked, "Is it true that Joey shot the last frame of the B-roll, Hawk?"

Hawk hesitated, then nodded slowly. "I was taking a break at the cafeteria while Joey played around with the camera," he told her. He gave her a level look, then went on, "But don't tell anyone. I don't want to get Joey in trouble."

"I won't," Nancy promised, then added, "Did Joey ever tell you about the shadow in the doorway of Katie's cage? He caught it on film at the end of the B-roll."

"Joey never mentioned it, but I noticed the shadow myself when I reviewed the B-roll later at the studio," Hawk replied.

"How did your ring get inside Katie's cage?" Nancy asked, seemingly out of the blue. "Did you film any of your shots from inside?"

"No way!" Hawk looked genuinely shocked. "I'm into tame little tabby cats, not great big wild ones!" he said. Then he looked at Nancy as he realized what she'd just said. "Wait. Are you saying that you found my ring *inside* Katie's cage?"

"Yes, Hawk. I already told you that."

"You did?" Hawk frowned, running his hand over his short black hair. "I was so excited to get it back, I guess I didn't hear you. Sorry." He took a deep breath, then added thoughtfully, "I have no idea how my ring ended up inside that cage. Maybe I flung it off by mistake. It is pretty loose on my finger."

Nancy decided to put a little more pressure on Hawk. She needed to see his reaction. "Your ring was inside Katie's cage, and I found it there on the same day her cubs were stolen," Nancy said. "Is that just a coincidence?"

Hawk started, looking at Nancy incredulously. Then he knitted his brows in a furious scowl. "Are you suggesting that I'm the thief? That's ridiculous. What would I want with four baby cougars?"

"You hate the idea of keeping animals cooped up in cages," Nancy said. "Maybe you just couldn't stand seeing the cubs in captivity."

Hawk sputtered for a moment, unable to get out his words. Then he leaned forward, pounding a tape deck with his fist.

"I may hate zoos," he said, his teeth clenched in fury, "but I would never steal newborn cougars away from their mother. What kind of creep do you take me for, anyway, Nancy?"

"You have to admit that the presence of your ring inside that cage is pretty incriminating. Plus, you don't seem to have an alibi for the time the one cub was moved outside the door, or for when the cubs were stolen. Maybe it was *your* shadow at the end of the B-roll."

Hawk's eyes glittered as he stared at Nancy. "I may not have alibis, but I do have a brain. Why don't you use yours for a moment? How would I have time to feed four newborn cubs every two hours with my work schedule lately? Have you noticed me sneaking out of the office? Besides, I spent four hours last night at dinner and the movies."

Nancy knew that Hawk could be right, and she also realized that he had met up with Joey soon after his brief absences at the zoo. She had to admit that there were a lot of problems with the theory that Hank was the thief.

Hawk drew himself up indignantly. "Plus, I would have needed keys to two locks: the nursery and the habitat gate. See?" he finished triumphantly. "Your circumstantial evidence would never stand up in court against me."

You could have an accomplice, Nancy thought, as if continuing the conversation. Someone who works at the zoo who shares your outrage at confining animals in zoos. You and your accomplice could be taking turns feeding the cubs before arranging to set them free in the wild. Hawk's voice broke into her thoughts.

"Now, if you're finished interrogating me, I've got work to do." Hawk shuffled some papers he was carrying.

"I'm finished," Nancy told him, rising from her chair. "And I'm sorry if I upset you. But your ring *was* in the cage, and I thought you might be able to tell me how it got there."

"Well, I can't," he said curtly, and walked out, slamming the door.

"Thanks for your time," Nancy said to the closed door. Next on the agenda, she decided, was to replay the B-roll one more time.

In the editing room, Linda Wong agreed to run the tape again. Nancy watched it carefully, but she came away knowing nothing more than when she went in.

Nancy headed toward Christy's office to replace the tape in her desk before Christy noticed it was gone. But Christy's office door was closed, and Christy was inside.

Nancy could hear Christy's shrill, angry tones through the door. She glanced up and down the empty corridor, then leaned closer. But no matter how hard she strained to listen, the only word she could hear Christy saying was "Vic."

Who's Vic? Nancy wondered. At that moment, Nancy heard Christy slam down her phone. Nancy backed away from the door just in time as Christy burst out of her office. Nancy watched Christy step into an elevator and the elevator doors close. Nancy quickly put the tape back under Christy's sweater and went to find George in the newsroom. George was gone, as were several reporters, and Nancy realized it was lunchtime.

Reluctantly, she decided to go home and grab some lunch, too.

Christy had said she'd be out of the office until three-thirty, Nancy remembered. After lunch she'd have time to check out Hawk's house *and* swing by the zoo to question both Eduardo and Junior Anderson.

At home Nancy ate a chicken sandwich made from Hannah's leftover roast, drank some iced tea, then changed into a light blue T-shirt, navy blue cotton leggings, and sneakers. Her eye caught a pair of binoculars on a hook in her closet. Perfect for observing animals—or humans—at the zoo, she thought as she placed them in her purse.

Nancy set off for Hawk's house and parked her Mustang in front of a trim brownstone in a refurbished section of River Heights. Standing in the alcove by the front door, Nancy studied the names next to three rows of buzzers and saw that T. Hawkins—Tom Hawkins was Hawk's full name—had the first-floor apartment.

Colorful petunias and geraniums sprouted from terra-cotta boxes at Hawk's windows. Peering over the flowers, Nancy saw a neatly kept bedroom and sitting room with a small, tidy kitchen in the back. There was no sign of cougars, big or little. But Hawk wasn't completely off the hook. The cubs could be at the home of his accomplice or in some other hiding place.

As Nancy drove away, she considered her other suspects: Eduardo Vallejo, Junior Anderson, and Christy. She couldn't stop thinking about what Christy and Eduardo were doing together last night at the zoo. Why had Christy denied being at the zoo and taking the B-roll? Could Eduardo have been the one to throw Nancy and Bess into the bat house?

And what about Junior Anderson? He was the only one who had a key whom she hadn't questioned yet—or even met. Nancy wasn't certain whether Junior had an alibi for the theft, but she thought she should talk to him before drawing any more conclusions about the case.

After parking her Mustang in a nearby lot, Nancy entered the zoo gates with a swarm of afternoon visitors. By now the day was oppressively hot. Nancy reached into her purse and took out a ponytail holder, then smoothed her hair back and fastened it.

Feeling cooler, she proceeded down the path by the administration offices. When the path forked three ways, she followed signs to the infirmary, which pointed down the walkway on the far left. Sally would know where to find Junior, Nancy reasoned.

Outside the infirmary, Nancy spotted Randy Thompson talking to an older man with white hair, a wizened face, and bright blue eyes. Nancy was about to say hi to Randy when the older man's loud voice abruptly stopped her.

"Eduardo took the cougars," the older man said to Randy. His gaze swept wildly around him as he spoke. "He's the thief—I'm sure of it!"

12

False Arrest

Nancy jolted to attention. Who was this man talking to Randy? she wondered. And why did he think that Eduardo was the thief?

At that moment Randy's eyes met Nancy's. His face broke into a warm smile. "Hi, Nancy. It's good to see you again. Have you met Junior Anderson?"

Nancy shook her head, then smiled at Junior. "You're just the person I was hoping to meet. I'm Nancy Drew."

Junior grunted, studying Nancy warily. His blue eyes looked flat as he appraised her under hooded lids.

Nancy smiled again, but Junior seemed to be immune to smiles. "I couldn't help overhearing you two talking," she said.

"I'm not surprised. We *were* pretty loud," Randy said, glaring at Junior.

Nancy, too, turned to look at Junior. "I'm curious. Why do you suspect Eduardo of stealing the cubs? Have you come across any evidence linking him with the theft?"

A corner of Junior's mouth twitched, then curled into a lopsided grin. "I don't *suspect* Eduardo—I *know* he stole those cubs," Junior declared. "With Eduardo, there's no need to fuss with evidence. His motive is enough to make any moron realize he's guilty."

Nancy perked up. "Motive? I didn't know he had a motive. What is it?"

"Nancy is investigating the theft of the cubs," Randy explained to Junior. "She's a detective."

"A detective?" Junior said, clearing his throat. He looked at Nancy with sudden interest. "Well, in that case, I'll be glad to tell you all about Eduardo Vallejo."

Nancy looked at Junior expectantly. "Eduardo comes from a famous circus family, the Courageous Vallejos," Junior said, as if he were relaying the latest gossip. "For generations the family has performed with big cats in the ring. Right now Eduardo's brother has a wild cat act that he tours around the country. But the brother"—Junior paused, and his eyes took on a gleam—"is about to go bankrupt."

"I didn't know any of this," Randy cut in. "Where'd you hear this gossip, Junior?"

"Gossip?" Junior said. "I prefer to call it 'information.' Eduardo and I have been colleagues at the zoo for a long time. Eduardo likes to talk. I can't help but listen."

Randy smiled at Nancy. "I guess I'm just not a part of the grapevine," he said with a modest shrug. "I never hear any of these things." He pushed back a lock of auburn hair that had fallen over his lightly tanned forehead. "I'm too busy with school and work and other stuff."

"I bet," Nancy said. Then she turned back to Junior. "Eduardo's brother is bankrupt?" she asked.

"He's on the verge of bankruptcy," Junior replied. "According to Eduardo, his brother has had a hard time finding trainable cats for his act."

"Why?" Nancy asked.

"Big cats are expensive," Junior replied. "And there aren't many available for sale. See, when they're born in a zoo, the zoo either keeps them or returns them to the wild. A zoo wouldn't be likely to sell them to the circus, for fear the animals wouldn't be treated right—depending on the circus, of course."

"So if a circus trainer was really desperate for some wild cats, stealing cougar cubs would be a real temptation," Nancy said.

Junior nodded. "And the best way to train a wild cat is to raise it from birth. These cubs would be a dream come true." Junior cupped his hand to his mouth in a conspiratorial way, then whispered, "I'm sure Eduardo stole those cougars. Aren't they just what his brother needs to make his act successful again?"

Nancy thought for a moment, then asked, "Were you anywhere near the cougar habitat when the theft happened?"

"Are you suggesting that *I* might have taken the cubs?" Junior asked petulantly. "Because if you are, I'm not going to answer you."

"I'm not suggesting any such thing," Nancy assured him. "I'm only curious to know if you heard or saw anything suspicious, that's all."

Junior relaxed a little. "I wish I had been, but right around the time the cubs were stolen, I was doing two feeding demonstrations—first the seals, and then the elephants—both in front of large audiences at the other end of the zoo." He sighed, then said, "Eduardo doesn't have an alibi."

"How do you know that?" Nancy asked.

"I just told you that Eduardo stole the cubs," Junior declared. "So, how could he have an alibi?"

Nancy raised her brows. Junior was certainly convinced that Eduardo was guilty, although his logic was a little simplistic, she thought. Was he right, or was he airing some sort of grudge? Nancy racked her brain for a way to get Eduardo to answer some of her questions.

Junior turned toward Randy. "It's bear-feeding

time. I'll see you around." Looking at Nancy, he added, "It's just a matter of time before Eduardo's charged with this crime. Take my word for it."

After Junior had moved out of earshot, Randy said, "He's quite a character. Because he's worked at the zoo for so long, he thinks he knows everything." Then he smiled. "And usually he's right."

"So you also think Eduardo took the cubs?" Nancy asked.

Randy shrugged. "I don't have any opinion either way. I just know that nine times out of ten, Junior's predictions are true." Randy glanced toward the infirmary, then shot Nancy an apologetic smile. "I should get back to work now, Nancy. I have to check out this tiger cub. He's been in the infirmary for a stomach bug, and I need to make sure he's putting on some weight again."

Nancy hesitated. She wanted to continue her investigation at the zoo, but she was tempted to ask Randy if she could see the tiger cub. A few extra minutes in the infirmary won't matter, she told herself.

"Would you mind if I take a look at the cub, too?" Nancy asked. "I'll bet he's adorable."

Randy grinned. "I'm sure the cub would love a visitor. Come on in."

Nancy followed Randy into the infirmary, which was built in the same attractive one-story stone style as the administration building and the animal cages.

Once inside, Randy drew a tranquilizer gun out of a cabinet and led Nancy to a line of cages against the far wall. A variety of animals—two monkeys, a koala bear, and several birds—rested inside the cages, but the alert tiger cub on the far left caught Nancy's eye.

"He doesn't look sick," she commented. The tiger was sprawled inside the cage, head up, watching her closely.

"He's ready to go back to his mother," Randy said. "I just want to weigh him first."

"How old is he?" Nancy asked.

"Six months. Usually we don't have to tranquilize such a young guy before handling him, but this cub's particularly feisty."

After waiting a few minutes for the tranquilizer to take effect, Randy opened the cage and lifted the heavy cub into his arms. Nancy was impressed with Randy's gentleness while he handled the cub. As Randy placed the limp body on the scale, the tiger's head fell back and his mouth dropped open.

"Look!" Nancy exclaimed. "He's missing one of his front teeth." She peered at another front tooth. It looked like a perfect match for the one in the threatening note she'd received.

"Tigers lose their baby teeth just the way human kids do," Randy explained. He wiggled the tiger's tooth. "See? This one's loose."

"What happens to the baby teeth once they fall out?" she asked. "I mean, I doubt there are tiger tooth fairies."

Randy grinned. "Teeth fall out in the cage or in the habitat, often when the animal is chewing on something," he explained. "If a tooth falls out in the cage, the tooth would be swept up during the daily cleaning. In the habitat, it's like any other organic matter—it would get blown away or buried, or it would eventually disintegrate."

So anyone with a key to the tiger habitat could have picked up the tooth. Nancy remembered Eduardo had been in the tiger habitat the day before.

Checking her watch, Nancy saw that it was already three o'clock. I'll have to track down Eduardo later, she thought reluctantly. It was time she returned to WRVH. Christy would be returning soon.

After saying goodbye to Randy, she walked quickly back toward her car.

Along the way, the sun beat steadily down through a thick hazy sky, and heat rose in waves from the asphalt path. The air was absolutely still. Nancy was thinking about how nice it would be to climb into her air-conditioned car when she noticed Sally Nelson buying an ice pop from a concession stand near the zoo entrance.

Nancy jogged over to her. "Hi, Sally. I was just at the infirmary." She told Sally about her visit with Randy.

"I'm glad that tiger's better," Sally said. "Randy's taken good care of him." She paused, then added, "So, what's on your agenda now, Nancy? Are you on your way out?" She nodded toward the gates.

"Yes," Nancy said. "I'm due back at work soon, but I couldn't resist doing a little detective work here first. And now, since I've run into you, Sally, would you mind if I asked you a few questions?"

"I wouldn't mind at all. Ask away. Why don't we talk on the way back to your car? That would save you some time."

The two young women strolled out between the zoo gates and headed down the sidewalk toward the parking lot.

"Bess and I were at the zoo last night," Nancy said, "and we saw Christy Kelley and Eduardo talking together. Do you have any idea why Christy would have been here so late?"

Sally looked puzzled. "Christy Kelley—your boss?" When Nancy nodded, Sally said, "I can't imagine what Christy was doing here after closing hours. I didn't realize she knew Eduardo."

"Neither did I—until last night. Does Eduardo often stay late?" Nancy asked. "It was past ten when we saw him."

"That's not unusual for Eduardo," Sally replied. "I've seen him here really late on a few occasions. He has no immediate family, and the big cats are his life—he's completely devoted to his job."

By now they'd reached Nancy's Mustang. Nancy unlocked it and opened her door. She was about to climb in when Sally jerked open the passenger-side door.

"What's this?" Sally said. She bent down and retrieved a baby bottle half filled with milk.

Nancy straightened. "Let me see."

"Wait." Sally opened the bottle and sniffed. Her head shot up, and she fixed Nancy with a penetrating stare. "It's formula used for baby felines! What's it doing in your car, Nancy?"

As Nancy stared at the bottle, a knot formed inside her stomach. "I don't know, Sally—honestly. Someone must have planted it there."

"And look, is this towel yours?" Sally bent down to pick up a bath towel from the front seat. It was covered with soft brown fur. "It's got cougar fur all over it." Sally gazed at Nancy, her lips pressed tightly together.

"I've never seen that towel before in my life," Nancy insisted. But Nancy had the feeling that Sally didn't believe her. "Look, Sally," Nancy went on. "I left my car windows open a bit because it's such a hot day. I bet someone pushed the bottle and the towel through the space." Nancy went around the car to demonstrate. Sure enough, the bottle and the towel fit through the crack. "I hope you believe me now," she said earnestly.

Sally's expression relaxed. "I didn't mean to doubt you, Nancy. But a bottle of feline formula and a towel covered with cougar fur are strange things to find in someone's car. You can't blame me for jumping to conclusions."

"Of course not. I'm sure whoever put them there was hoping that someone would do just that."

Sally took the bottle and towel from Nancy. "Do you mind if I keep these and show them to Richard?"

"Not at all," Nancy replied calmly. But despite her confident manner, she felt rattled by the incident. She hoped Dr. Annenberg would realize that someone had set her up.

After saying goodbye to Sally, Nancy drove through downtown River Heights toward the WRVH building. A block away from the station, she saw a pet store and got an idea. She parked the Mustang by the curb, then headed inside the store.

The interior was brightly lit, with pet supplies neatly hung on racks. A stern-looking man was seated behind the counter. His piercing gray eyes never blinked as he stared at Nancy.

"Hello," she said, smiling uneasily. "I wonder if you could help me. Has anyone been in here recently asking about wild cat care?"

"Wild cat care?" The man's head shot forward like a snapping turtle's. Then, to Nancy's amazement, he grabbed something and came around the counter, positioning himself between her and the door. In one hand he brandished a huge butcher knife, its blade glinting menacingly under the bright overhead lights. Before Nancy could react, he slashed it once through the air, then pointed it menacingly at her.

"Don't move, Nancy Drew!" he shouted. "I'm calling the police!"

13

Poisoned!

Nancy didn't move. With the sharp point of the knife blade almost touching her, she didn't want to provoke the man any further. As calmly as she could, she asked, "Why are you calling the police?"

"You know perfectly well why. Don't play games with me!" he bellowed at her harshly, his eyes blazing with anger.

Nancy flinched. "I honestly don't know. There must be some mistake."

"I don't make mistakes, Miss Drew," the man snarled. "You stole those baby cougars, and you're not getting away with the crime."

Nancy gasped. "You're mistaken. I *am* Nancy Drew, but I didn't steal the cougars."

"I told you, I don't make mistakes," the man said.

Nancy knew that Chief McGinnis from the River Heights Police Department would be able to set the man straight. Nancy and Chief McGinnis had worked together on many cases. He wouldn't hesitate to vouch for her.

"If you'll put away your knife and call the police," Nancy said, "Chief McGinnis will clear up this misunderstanding. I promise I won't run."

The man cocked his head and frowned. Nancy guessed he was trying to decide whether to believe her. After a long moment, he lowered the knife. "Sit on the stool here behind the counter until the police come," he commanded. "And no funny stuff—or else." He whipped his knife through the air in a dramatic gesture.

This man is crazy, Nancy thought, keeping her eyes on the knife anxiously as she sat down. *And it's creepy that he knows my name.* But Nancy knew it would be better not to ask him to explain.

After muttering a few words into the phone, the man leaned against the wall, folded his arms across his chest, and glared at Nancy.

Ten minutes of awkward silence passed.

The bell above the entrance rang. "Hi, Nancy," a friendly voice said. Nancy swiveled around and saw a young dark-haired policeman walking through the door of the shop.

"Officer Rao!" she exclaimed. "I'm so happy you're here."

"I'll bet," Officer Rao said, smiling at Nancy.

"I'm handing the culprit over to you, Officer," the store owner said, gesturing grandly toward Nancy. "This young lady here is the one you're looking for. I trust those cubs can be returned to their mother now and that this crime will be prosecuted to the fullest extent of the law."

"Why are you so sure I'm the thief?" Nancy finally asked the man. "And why did you threaten me with a knife?"

"The officer here will tell you how I *know* you're the thief," the man said. "As for the knife, I didn't want you to run away."

"You threatened Nancy with a knife?" Officer Rao looked startled. "Look, sir," he said sternly. "The police department appreciates your help, but there was absolutely no need to take matters into your own hands like that. I'm afraid we'll have to issue you a warning."

The store owner blanched, then apologized profusely to Officer Rao. "I . . . I was just trying to help," he said.

"Don't apologize to me," Officer Rao snapped. "Apologize to Nancy. I'll take that knife, if you please, and I'll return later to discuss this incident further with you."

The pet store owner mumbled an apology and handed the knife over, but he never stopped glaring at Nancy.

Officer Rao led Nancy outside. "I'm sorry about what happened in there, Nancy. Are you okay?" he asked.

Nancy nodded. "Yes, but I'm glad you're giving that guy a warning. For a few minutes there, I thought he was actually going to use that knife on me."

"I'm going to drive you back to police headquarters," Officer Rao explained, opening the door to his squad car for her. "Chief McGinnis has a few questions for you."

Nancy climbed into the car, wondering what Chief McGinnis wanted to ask her. "So why did the pet store owner think I'm the one who stole the cougars?" she asked Officer Rao as they drove toward headquarters.

"You mean you *didn't* take the cougars?" Officer Rao joked, the angles in his face softening. "Don't worry, Nancy," he went on in a more serious tone. "We know that you didn't steal the cougars."

"Gee, thanks," Nancy said.

"The police asked all pet store owners around town to call headquarters if anyone came in with questions relating at all to the cougarnapping. I guess that man went overboard when you came in and started asking questions."

"You're not kidding," Nancy agreed.

"Then this morning," the officer continued, "someone fitting your description and calling herself Nancy Drew was reported seen at several local pet stores looking for baby formula for large cats."

"What? Someone calling herself Nancy Drew?" Nancy repeated, stunned. "Who could that have been?"

"That's exactly what we'd like to find out." Officer Rao pulled up beside the police station.

Officer Rao led Nancy to Chief McGinnis's office, then waved goodbye. After getting a warm greeting from Chief McGinnis, Nancy sat down in a chair opposite him.

"Nancy," Chief McGinnis began, giving Nancy a level look from across his desk, "I know you didn't steal the cougar cubs. But someone is trying to frame you. Just now we got a call from the zoo suggesting you as a suspect."

Nancy sat bolt upright. Someone from the zoo suspected her of the theft? Trying to keep her voice steady, she asked, "Who called?"

Chief McGinnis dropped his gaze. "Sally Nelson, the veterinarian, said she found a bottle of cougar formula and a towel with some cougar fur on it in your car. She said she felt bad about reporting you, but she couldn't ignore what she'd found."

"But I told her someone planted them in my car." Nancy moaned. "I guess she didn't believe me." After a moment she added, "I hope you believe me, Chief McGinnis."

Chief McGinnis smiled. "Of course I believe you, Nancy. I've known you too long to doubt you for even a second. But I want you to be careful," he warned. "Those mysterious visits to pet shops and that bottle of formula in your car indicate to me that someone wants you to take the rap for the crime."

"Someone fitting my description," Nancy said thoughtfully.

Chief McGinnis nodded. "It could be the real cougar thief, or just some wacko who bears a grudge against you. In either case, we'll find her."

Nancy told the chief about all the threats she'd had: the cobra, the note, and the attacks at the zoo. But she decided not to mention any of her suspects yet. She was worried that if the police zeroed in on the thief, he or she might flee with the cougars.

"Be careful, Nancy," Chief McGinnis warned again. "This thief is clearly dangerous."

"I will, Chief McGinnis," Nancy promised. "Thanks for your information, and I'll keep you up to date on what I find out, too."

On the way back to WRVH in Officer Rao's squad car, Nancy mulled over what Chief McGinnis had told her. Someone fitting her description and calling herself Nancy Drew was asking pet stores about cougar care. Christy Kelley looked like her. And Christy had been out of the office until late morning. She could have been going around to pet stores then.

The images of Christy talking to Eduardo at

the zoo the previous night, then the B-roll hidden in Christy's drawer, flashed through Nancy's mind. But Christy had an alibi for when the cougars were stolen—Nancy had seen her with her own eyes at WRVH. But Christy could be working with Eduardo or with Hawk.

Officer Rao dropped Nancy off outside the pet store, where she had left her car. She drove over to the WRVH building and parked in the lot, still thinking about Christy and all the questions she had for her.

As Nancy jogged up the flight of stairs that led to the building door, she checked her watch again. It was almost five o'clock. I hope Christy's still around, she thought.

Before Nancy could take another step, though, George rushed out of the building, nearly colliding with her.

"Nancy!" George shouted, her face pale. "I'm so glad you're back." She stared at Nancy, gulping in breaths.

"What's the matter, George?" Nancy asked, instantly imagining terrible things.

George's voice shook as she replied, and her sentences were punctuated by gulps of air. "Christy's in the hospital—fighting for her life. Someone poisoned her lunch."

14

What's in a Name?

Shocked, Nancy took a step backward, nearly losing her balance on the stairs.

"Careful, Nancy," George said, grabbing her arm. "We don't want you in the hospital, too."

"You and me both." Nancy paused, gathering her thoughts. Christy, who had become one of Nancy's main suspects, had been poisoned. What was going on? "Christy's life is really in danger?" Nancy asked.

"The doctors are very worried," George said gravely. "I went out for lunch and then to the library for Christy, so I'm not exactly sure what happened. By the time I got back, the ambulance had come and gone. I was just leaving to track you down, since I knew you'd want to hear about all this."

Nancy was silent as she considered the afternoon's chain of events, ending with the attempt on Christy's life. What did the events have to do with the missing cougars—if anything? Nancy felt a twinge of fear. Whoever poisoned Christy obviously meant business.

Nancy filled George in on her own investigation that afternoon, including the incident at the pet supply store and her suspicions that Christy had framed her.

"She *must* be involved in the cougar theft somehow," Nancy said. "But how?" She paused for a moment, then added, "By the way, what happened this morning when you lured Christy into the newsroom while I searched her office?"

"Boy, did I get a lucky break," George said. "Mr. Liski came along before we even got to the newsroom. He asked Christy to meet with him for a moment about a possible story idea. That's the last time I saw her."

"I think the first thing we should do is question WRVH employees," Nancy said as she led George back inside the building. "We need more information about what Christy ate and where she bought the food if we expect to find any clues about who poisoned her. I'll bet that if we find the poisoner, we're closer to finding Christy's partner in the cougar theft."

The two girls headed up to the newsroom in

the elevator. Upstairs, a throng of employees waited for the elevators.

"It's five o'clock—time to leave," George observed as people packed into the elevator she and Nancy had just exited. "I hope we'll find enough people to question."

"Are you kidding?" Nancy said. "People work around the clock at a TV station. You can't leave in the middle of a groundbreaking story."

"Some people can," George muttered as more employees surged into the hallway. "But look, there's Linda Wong. Maybe she'll agree to talk for a moment."

Nancy walked up to the film editor strolling through the vestibule and asked her if she had a moment to talk.

"I'm not leaving for a while, Nancy," Linda assured her. "I was just passing through here after a meeting with Hawk."

Good, Nancy thought—Hawk's still around. She made a mental note to question him, too.

After Nancy and George followed Linda into her editing room, Nancy said, "George just told me about Christy. Have you heard any more news about how she's doing?"

"Not really," Linda answered. "I just know that the doctors are worried about her. She's unconscious, you know."

"That's awful," Nancy said. "I remember Christy's saying that she was going out for lunch. . . . I wonder if the doctors learned any details from her about the poisoning, like where she ate?"

Linda shrugged. "I saw her come into the building around two-thirty with a paper bag. I assumed it was her lunch. I saw her eating a sandwich at her desk a little later."

"Does anyone know where she bought it?" George asked.

"No one knows whether Christy brought her lunch from home or bought it at a sandwich shop," Linda said. "Sometimes she brings a sandwich or salad from home when she doesn't have a business lunch scheduled."

"Could the doctors identify the poison?" Nancy asked.

Linda nodded as she pushed back a lock of her long dark hair. "The hospital lab traced the poison to her sandwich. It was turkey with ratugula greens—"

"You mean arugula leaves?" Nancy asked.

"No. Ratugula," Linda said emphatically. "It looks a lot like lettuce, but it's a deadly poison."

Nancy asked Linda the name of the hospital where Christy had been admitted, and then she and George went in search of Hawk. At the elevator bank, the two girls ran into Joey. Nancy asked him if Hawk was still at work.

"He left about ten minutes ago," Joey told them. "I'm calling it a day, too. Hey—would you guys like to get a soda or cappuccino or something?"

"No thanks," Nancy said. "George and I have an errand to do. Maybe some other day."

Just then an elevator door slid open. As Nancy, George, and Joey rode downstairs, Nancy asked, "Do you know whether Hawk was at WRVH all day today, Joey?"

"He was here this morning, but at lunchtime we went out to shoot a story—we got back here only an hour ago."

So Hawk probably wasn't involved in the poisoning, Nancy concluded.

The elevator doors opened. "Well, see you around," Joey said as they all trooped out of the building.

Nancy and George waved good-bye to him, then walked to Nancy's Mustang. After buckling her seat belt, Nancy turned to George, her face bright with excitement.

"Uh-oh," George groaned. "I know that look on your face, Drew. What are we going to check out now?"

"Christy's house, of course," Nancy said.

George rolled her eyes. "I should have agreed to go out with Joey. But I guess it makes sense to see whether Christy has ratugula leaves in her fridge."

Nancy looked up Christy's address in a pocket directory of WRVH employees. Then she drove through River Heights to a leafy suburb of stone and clapboard houses with wraparound porches and wide front yards. Shaded by a large oak tree, Christy's white clapboard house was small but well kept, with rows of begonias lining the brick walkway to the porch. The scent of boxwood bushes wafted through the humid afternoon air.

At the front door, Nancy quickly slipped a credit card from her purse. With a quick glance around, to make sure none of the neighbors was watching, she eased the lock open. Once inside, Nancy and George stopped short in surprise.

"Are you sure this is Christy's house?" George asked. "I mean, her office is always super neat."

"And this is a megamess," Nancy said, taking in the knocked-down furniture and shredded papers scattered everywhere. The house felt stuffy and hot, and the air smelled sour. Nancy picked up a bottle of white liquid on the floor and sniffed inside. "George, I'm absolutely sure this is Christy's house," she declared, wrinkling her nose. "Christy's got to be the look-alike who tried to frame me. These bottles have feline formula in them. She must have been the one to put a bottle and that towel in my car."

"Look at all of them!" George exclaimed as she and Nancy walked into the kitchen. The counters and floor were strewn with bottles of cougar formula—some partly filled, others empty. Nancy opened the refrigerator. Unused bottles filled with formula were stacked on the shelves, but there were no greens of any kind in the crisper.

Nancy and George wandered back into the living room. In the corner was a plaid dog bed covered with tawny fur. Nancy stooped down and picked up a tuft. It felt soft as she rubbed it between her fingers.

"So Christy must have stolen the cougars," George said. "But how did she do it, and why?"

"And even more important—where are the cougars now?" Nancy said. Nancy had a horrible feeling that whoever poisoned Christy had taken the cubs and run.

Nancy and George made a futile search of the rest of the house. Christy might not be the easiest person to work for, Nancy mused, but was she really capable of stealing newborn cubs? Christy had an alibi for when the cubs were taken. She had been driving Nancy and George to the zoo. So how had the cubs ended up in her house?

Scanning the living room one more time, Nancy felt sure that Christy had been a willing party to the crime. The bottles and cougar fur were evidence that Christy had been caring for the cubs in her house, and her attendance at work had been patchy lately. But who was her accomplice? Nancy wondered. Who had actually taken the cubs from the zoo?

George pointed to a heart-shaped pillow on the sofa. "I didn't know Christy had a mushy side," she said dryly.

Nancy smiled as she picked up the pillow. On the white fabric, the initials *CK* and *VT* were embroidered in pink thread. "I didn't know she had a criminal side, either," Nancy said, gazing at the messy room, "till now."

Nancy placed the pillow back against the sofa cushion, then glanced toward the front door. Sunlight slanted low through the fan-shaped window above the door, casting deep shadows along the varnished wood floor.

"George," Nancy said, "it's getting late. Let's drive over to the zoo, pronto. If Eduardo's still at work, I'd like to follow him. Christy *must* have an accomplice—a zoo worker, I'm sure—someone who has keys and feels comfortable with wild animals. Eduardo's the most likely suspect. He and Christy seemed pretty friendly last night. I have a hunch he might lead us to the cougars."

"I'm all for indulging your hunches, Nan," George said agreeably. "Lead on."

It was past six o'clock when Nancy and George arrived at the zoo gates. After making a quick phone call to Dr. Annenberg's office, the security guard let Nancy and George inside. "Why don't we ask Dr. Annenberg for Eduardo's home address? That way we won't have to follow him—we can go straight to his house."

Nancy agreed, and she and George strode down the path to the administration building. Along the way, where the path curved sharply to the left, Nancy heard a man's voice raised in anger. It came from beyond some foliage bordering the pathway. "It's Eduardo!" she said, grabbing George's arm. "He sounds furious."

"I take perfect care of my cats, I tell you!" Eduardo shouted. "How dare you doubt my expertise?"

"Who's he arguing with?" George asked, as a deeper male voice resonated down the path.

Nancy instantly recognized Junior Anderson's gravelly voice, but she couldn't hear his words. "It's Junior Anderson, the guy who feeds the animals. Let's get closer."

Nancy and George crept forward and peered around the curve. Junior and Eduardo were quarreling no more than five feet away. Just then a twig snapped under Nancy's sneaker. The two men immediately hushed as they saw Nancy and George.

"I remember you," Junior said to Nancy. "You're Randy Thompson's friend."

"Yes, I know him—" Nancy began.

"You'll have to excuse me. I've got some animals to feed," Junior cut in. He scowled at Eduardo. "We'll continue this discussion some other time." He shuffled away down the path.

"That man infuriates me," Eduardo sputtered as beads of perspiration rolled down his forehead. "He's never been nice to me in all the years I've worked here. He calls into question my training methods, my dedication, everything. I love my job, but I cannot stand another moment working with him!"

"Why does he treat you that way?" Nancy asked.

Eduardo's eyes snapped with fury. "He bears an unfair grudge against me. Years ago, he tried to get the job as cat keeper. But the zoo hired *me.*"

"And he's never let you hear the end of it?" George asked.

"Never," Eduardo proclaimed.

Could Junior be blaming Eduardo for the catnapping because of this grudge? Nancy wondered. But if Eduardo was innocent, then who could Christy's accomplice be? Hawk was an unlikely suspect at this point, since neither he nor Christy had keys to Katie's cage.

But despite her sudden doubts about Eduardo, Nancy felt it was still worth searching his house while he was busy at the zoo.

"I have to go now, George," Nancy said pointedly, nudging George's foot with her sneaker.

Taking the hint, George said goodbye to Eduardo, then she and Nancy walked briskly down the path to the administration offices.

Inside Dr. Annenberg's office, his secretary moved aside to allow Nancy and George access to a computer where an alphabetized list of zoo employees was kept on file.

Nancy clicked on the computer, then called up the file. With her finger on the cursor key, she ran quickly through the file until she reached employee names beginning with *V*. "I've got it," she announced. "Eduardo Vallejo—I think it's the only *V* name here."

Glancing up the list to make sure, Nancy suddenly stopped. The name above Eduardo's flashed out at her like a neon sign.

15

Prince Stalks His Prey

Nancy whirled toward George, her eyes bright with excitement. "I just figured something out," she said.

George waited for her to explain.

Nancy pointed to the computer screen. "Look at the name above Eduardo's."

George gazed at the screen and then back at Nancy. "Randy Thompson?" she said with a puzzled frown. "The assistant vet whom Bess has a crush on? What about him?"

"Randy *Victor* Thompson," Nancy explained. "Don't you remember the initials on Christy's heart-shaped pillow?"

"Yes . . ." George nodded thoughtfully.

"Christy had an argument on the phone earlier today," Nancy added. "Her office door was shut, and the only word I caught was 'Vic.' Maybe Christy calls Randy by his middle name!"

"So the initials *VT* on Christy's pillow might stand for Vic Thompson," George murmured.

Nancy nodded. "A.k.a. Randy. I'll bet he's Christy's boyfriend—and her accomplice in crime." Nancy opened her purse and brought out the sunglasses she'd found in the cougar habitat. She showed George the *V* between the smudges. "These glasses must belong to Randy."

"Yeah, but Randy could have dropped them in the cougar habitat before the theft," George pointed out.

"That's true, but take another look at the computer." Once again Nancy pointed to the computer monitor.

"So?" George said with a shrug. "You're showing me Randy's address, but what about it?"

"Randy's address is 117 Oak Street," Nancy replied. "And Oak Street runs behind the cougar habitat. There's a gate in the back wall. Randy could have taken the cubs through it, straight across the street to his house."

"I'm not sticking up for Randy," George said, "but I'm still not convinced he's Christy's accomplice. Wasn't he taking a vet-school exam when the cougars were stolen?"

"We can call the school and see," Nancy said.

Dr. Annenberg strode into the room. "Hello," he said. "Making any progress?"

"Maybe," Nancy said. "But I need your help."

Without explaining her suspicions, Nancy asked Dr. Annenberg if he knew the name of Randy's vet-school professor—the one who'd given the exam.

"Hmm," Dr. Annenberg said. "Randy told me he was taking Anatomy of Mammals. I have a friend who teaches at the school. I'm sure he knows who's teaching that class." Dr. Annenberg disappeared into his private office and, five minutes later, emerged with the information Nancy needed.

"Dr. Ida Campbell is the professor," Dr. Annenberg said, handing Nancy a slip of paper with the name and a phone number on it.

"Thanks, Dr. Annenberg," Nancy said as he left for the day.

Nancy quickly dialed the professor's number and had a brief conversation with her.

"Well, George," she said, hanging up, "Professor Campbell told me she *didn't* give an exam yesterday. So why would Randy lie, unless he had something big to hide?"

George shook her head. "Boy, Bess is going to have to get over Randy fast after this news." She paused, then added, "But how do you explain Christy's being poisoned? Would her boyfriend poison her?"

"Good point," Nancy admitted. "Maybe they had a fight about what to do with the cubs."

"Why would Randy and Christy even want the cubs in the first place?" George asked.

Nancy remembered Sally's mentioning the black market for endangered animals. "Vet school is about as expensive as medical school. I wonder if Randy plans to sell the cubs for tuition money."

"And Christy's helping out?" George said.

"Either that, or maybe Randy offered to split the money with her. Maybe they argued about money and that's why he poisoned her." Nancy rose from her chair. "But I don't think we should sit around here guessing. Let's head over to Randy's house. I'll bet it's directly behind the zoo wall."

Ten minutes later Nancy and George were standing outside 117 Oak Street. True to Nancy's prediction, the small brick apartment building was across the street from the back wall of the zoo. A half a block away, the gate in the stone wall led to the cougar habitat.

Nancy and George gazed at the building. By now, the evening sky was a velvety black, but the heat of the day lingered. Not a breath of air stirred the oak and maple trees lining the quiet street.

"I can't believe how hot it is," Nancy commented. She studied the dark windows on the first floor, shut up tight. "If the cubs are inside, they must be roasting."

"Looks like no one's home," George said. "Randy might have already sold the cubs."

"We'd better check," Nancy urged. She and

George circled the building, trying to look in, but the curtains were drawn across all the windows on the bottom floor. Frustrated, Nancy peered up at the windows on the second floor.

"There's a dim light on upstairs," Nancy said. "Would you stand guard here, George, while I climb the zoo wall across the street? I might be able to see inside if I use my binoculars."

"Shouldn't I come with you?" George asked.

Nancy shook her head. "You'd better stay here in case Randy sneaks in or out with the cougars. If you hide near the side of the building, he won't see you from the front yard."

George agreed, and Nancy crossed Oak Street to the sidewalk running along the eight-foot-high zoo wall. Nancy scanned the wall in both directions and found a nearby apple tree with branches that scraped its top. Shouldering her purse, she scrambled up the tree and onto the wall. Nancy glanced uneasily into the cougar habitat beneath her on the far side of the wall. All she saw was darkness and the denser darkness of trees and rocks.

Straddling the wall, she took her binoculars from her purse and held them before her eyes. There was a narrow gap in the curtains that hung in the window on the left.

A thrill went through Nancy. The far corner of a room was lit softly by a hallway light behind it. Nancy could just make out a plaid dog bed like the one at Christy's house. On it were four baby cougars cuddled together, sleeping peacefully.

Nancy was about to jump down, to tell George about what she'd seen, when an unearthly noise—part growl, part screech—rose from below. Adrenaline shot down Nancy's spine.

It's Prince, she realized—Katie's mate. He was prowling in the darkness below her.

Nancy looked down at the habitat. The section of it near the wall was dense with foliage—bushes, long grass, and scrub pines. Once more, Prince's cry echoed eerily through the night air. Peering through her binoculars, Nancy tried to locate him. The waning moon gave off a weak silvery light, and Nancy was hoping the cougar's eyes might reflect it. She leaned forward, scanning the shrubbery, but there was no sign of Prince.

Suddenly, Nancy felt something push her from behind. Her binoculars and purse catapulted into the cougar habitat while she struggled to keep her balance, desperately clawing at the wall. The rough stones scraped her fingers as she fell, but somehow she managed to hold on with one hand.

Nancy glanced upward, searching the darkness for a place to hold on with her other hand.

But before Nancy knew what was happening, a hand shot over the top of the wall from the other side and struck her own hand with terrible force.

Nancy cried out as a sharp pain shot through her fingers. She couldn't hold on.

A second later she landed with a thud on a soft patch of earth between two large bushes in the cougar habitat.

Nancy knew she had only seconds to act. Prince was prowling somewhere nearby. Even though Nancy remembered that cougars rarely attack people, she also knew that they were nocturnal and hunted their prey at night. She didn't want to be a late-night snack for the fierce animal.

Prince roared, the sound ripping through the night. Fear shot through Nancy. Her gaze swept the foliage around her. Once more, he cried out—the sound wild and terrifying—but she couldn't pinpoint the location. The noise seemed to rise from the entire habitat.

Then she saw a glint in the dark. About forty feet away, the moonlight glanced off a pair of wild-looking yellow eyes. It was Prince, stalking her from a cluster of trees.

The great cat stared at Nancy for a moment, then leaped forward. Desperately, Nancy swiveled around and hugged the wall, knowing there was no way she could outrun him. She braced herself, expecting to feel the claws of the animal tearing through her skin.

16

Home Sweet Home

Suddenly, Nancy found herself in motion, running for her life. At the same time, a single word rang in her head: water. She had remembered Bess saying that moats surrounded the cat habitats because wild cats don't like water any more than do house cats. If she could make it to the nearest moat, Prince probably wouldn't follow her into the water.

Dodging trees and rocks, she raced onward, close to the wall on her right.

C'mon, Drew, she urged herself, you'll get there. Run just a little faster!

Her breath came in ragged gasps as her sneakers scudded through the dusty earth. Her lungs felt as if they were on fire, and her chest heaved as she struggled to keep up her speed. Just when she thought she could hold out no longer, she broke out from the underbrush and saw a dark patch spread out before her. It was a man-made river, a moat, the water as still as ice on the hot night.

She dashed toward it. The paws of the great beast thundered behind her. Would she make it before he caught her? Her legs felt like jelly as she made one final sprint toward the water. Nancy gulped in a breath, then leaped into the black liquid.

She thankfully felt the cool water surround her as she plunged deep and swam underwater as far away from Prince as she could get. When she finally came up for air, she shot a quick look toward shore behind her. Prince stood by the water, his eyes fixed on hers, then turned nonchalantly and disappeared into a nearby grove of trees.

Nancy closed her eyes in relief. She was safe.

But suddenly there was a loud splash behind her. Nancy whirled around as a dark figure lunged toward her. Before she had time to react, she was pushed forward, her face shoved under the water.

Nancy began to choke as water trickled down her throat. She tried to lift her head, but her attacker's grip was too tight. Her heart pumped furiously, and her lungs felt as if they would burst. In a few more seconds, she would drown!

Nancy flailed about, desperately trying to free

herself. Her arm swung into her attacker, knocking him loose. As he released his hold on her, Nancy shot up in the water. Gasping for air, she grabbed her assailant's shoulder. With a judo move slowed by the water, she managed to push him down into the moat.

Her chest still heaving, Nancy gazed at the water. The startled face of Randy Thompson stared up at her from the dark surface.

Suddenly, a voice boomed from the edge of the moat, "The police have been called. They're on their way!"

Nancy recognized Eduardo's voice. "Help!" she shouted. "Eduardo! Help me!"

A splashing sound alerted Nancy. Randy was escaping! He was swimming furiously toward the far shore—the unoccupied habitat next to the cougars.

Nancy took off after him, but she was too slow. He was already climbing out of the moat.

"Eduardo!" Nancy screamed. "Randy's at the moat. He's getting away!"

Randy was stumbling to his feet just as Eduardo burst from the darkness and landed a punch squarely on his jaw. With a low moan, Randy fell backward to the ground.

Nancy struggled through the water to help Eduardo, but every movement seemed to be in slow motion. Finally, she reached the bank. Water poured off her clothes, and her wet sneakers made a squelching sound as she climbed out.

"Here!" Eduardo cried, throwing Nancy some rope. "I'll hold him down while you tie his hands behind him."

Nancy worked quickly while Eduardo gripped Randy in a wrestler's choke hold.

"That should hold him until the police come," Nancy said as she finished. She looked up gratefully at Eduardo. "It's lucky you were around tonight, Eduardo. Did you just happen to hear us struggling in the moat?"

"Your friend alerted me," Eduardo explained. "The tall, dark-haired girl named George. I was making my final nightly rounds to make sure all my cats were settled. Your friend spotted me from the gate in the wall and yelled. Thank goodness I had my cell phone with me." He patted his shirt pocket.

Way to go, George, Nancy thought gratefully.

Randy stirred. Turning his head toward Nancy, he growled, "You ruined everything for me, you rotten snoop. If you hadn't interfered—"

"If I hadn't interfered, you would have sold the cougars on the black market to get money for vet school," Nancy said.

Surprise darted across Randy's face. But it was quickly replaced by a nasty sneer. "You think you're pretty smart, Nancy Drew."

"And Christy didn't know who she was dealing with when she helped you," Nancy shot back. "You poisoned her, didn't you?"

Randy scowled. "Leave her out of this."

"Tell me," Nancy went on, "did you put Hawk's ring inside Katie's cage, too?"

"I found a ring with a hawk on it, yeah," Randy admitted. "I threw it in, just to throw busybodies like you off my scent. I was happier about it when I heard it belonged to that cameraman. He nearly gave me a heart attack the first time I went to take the cubs. There he was—filming!"

"You're a fool, Randy Victor Thompson," Nancy said. "The man who almost got you on film was not the man whose ring you threw into Katie's cage."

Randy snorted. "So what? They both got in my way, so I had to make a second try. Thanks to them, Katie sensed that something was up, so the next time I had to use the tranquilizers."

Eduardo snorted. "Katie's a cat. Her instincts are sharp enough to smell a rat like you."

Nancy grinned at Eduardo, then turned back to Randy. "So finally you got the chance to take the cubs to your house through the back gate. But how did you manage to care for them?"

"I have my ways," Randy said smugly. "I'd been preparing for this theft by stealing small amounts of formula, little by little, from the zoo infirmary."

"So how did the cougars end up at Christy's house?" Nancy asked. "Did you stick her with their care?"

"No," Randy snapped. "I was fair to Christy.

She took two cubs and I took two. It was the only way we could manage with our busy jobs, since the sale wouldn't take place for several more days."

"Why did you poison Christy?" Nancy asked.

Randy glared at her. "That is none of your business."

"Well, then, what about the snake?" Nancy demanded. "Did you plant him on my car? That *is* my business."

"That was cool." Randy couldn't seem to resist bragging. "I was hiding out, keeping my alibi clean, when I overheard you tell your friend that you were going to investigate what had happened to the first cougar. I thought a little visit from Stanley might dissuade you. But, no, Nancy Drew is too tough for that.

"And, Nancy, in case you're still clueless, I sabotaged the monorail, too. 'What a wonderful idea! I'll get to case the whole zoo!'" Randy mimicked Nancy's enthusiasm for the ride he had suggested. "Just a little steel bar across the track, and crash! I bet you'll have hyena nightmares for years. Bats, too, I bet. Eee-eee-eee!" Randy's voice sounded eerily just like the bats. "That was me! That was me, too!"

The piercing sound of a police siren wailed through the night. Randy looked toward the habitat gate as two squad cars appeared on the asphalt path outside.

Dr. Annenberg unlocked the gate, and Officer Rao and three of his colleagues rushed through and headed straight for them.

Within seconds the police handcuffed Randy and led him away. Nancy and Eduardo strolled back to the gate together behind the police.

"I have one question for you, Eduardo," Nancy said. "What were you and Christy doing together at the zoo last night?"

Eduardo gave her a quizzical look. "Christy? You mean Randy's accomplice you were speaking of? I don't believe I've ever met her."

Nancy described what Christy looked like and Eduardo remembered. "Ah, the woman who looks a little bit like you, Nancy. I was at the zoo late last night—as usual—and I came upon her. At first I thought she was you, but then I saw differently. She said she'd come for equipment her camera crew had left behind. I accepted her explanation, and we parted ways. She tracked me down a moment later to ask if I'd let her out the main entrance, which I did."

Christy was still a mystery to Nancy. A liar, yes, but Nancy had a feeling she wasn't the cold-hearted animal kidnapper that Randy was. Nancy felt a tug of anxiety in her stomach—or maybe it was hunger. In any case, she made a mental note to call the hospital as soon as she got home.

The next day, Saturday, dawned sunny and crisp. Nancy, George, Bess, Hawk, and Joey were sitting at the zoo café, eating brunch, when Sally strolled by on her way to the infirmary.

"You'll have to stop by the nursery later, Nancy," she said. "Katie wants to thank you."

After Nancy promised she would, Sally said, "By the way, Nancy, I'm sorry I called the police about the bottle of formula and the towel that were in your car. I feel really bad about that."

"Don't worry about it, Sally," Nancy said. "I feel bad about suspecting Hawk and Eduardo." She smiled at Hawk apologetically, then turned back to Sally. "I was just telling my friends that I visited Christy at the hospital this morning. She's much better, and she was able to tell me more about the cougar theft."

"Was Christy the one who put the bottle of formula in your car?" Sally asked.

Nancy nodded. "She was trying to frame me. That's why she pretended to be me at pet stores and asked the salespeople how to care for wild cats."

"I'd like to hear more later," Sally said, "but I have to go back to Katie to make sure her cubs are nursing well. When we collected them from Randy's house last night, they were a little hungry but generally in good health."

After Sally left, George said, "You were just beginning to tell us about Christy—that she's better, but she won't be going back to WRVH any time soon. So then what?"

Putting down her orange juice, Nancy explained, "Christy will be prosecuted as Randy's accomplice in the theft of the baby cougars. But she'll get a lighter sentence if she testifies against him."

"I suppose he *was* her boyfriend," Bess said, making a face. "What a rat. I'll bet she feels stupid falling for him."

George laughed. "I seem to remember someone else falling for Randy—not so long ago."

"Don't remind me," Bess said, blushing. "I guess that old saying really is true: love is blind. But don't worry, more waffles will help me forget I ever had a crush on that guy."

As Bess signaled to the waiter, Nancy explained to the others that Christy still called Randy by his former nickname, Vic.

"So how did Christy help Randy with the theft?" Joey asked Nancy.

"Not only did she look after two of the cubs but she also lifted the incriminating B-roll of film from Linda's files. And she was the one who put the threatening note that Randy had written into my purse when I got back to the network after the shoot."

"Christy must have been pretty devoted to Randy to help him out with his scheme," Hawk commented, putting down his coffee cup. "Did he offer to split the money with her?"

"No," Nancy said. "At first Christy didn't even realize he was planning to sell the cubs. Randy roped her into the scheme by offering to kidnap the cubs and let Christy find them—in some abandoned warehouse downtown. Then she'd earn all this glory as an investigator."

"Yeah, right!" Joey said sarcastically. "So, whose idea was it to frame you?"

"Randy's," Nancy replied. "But Christy really liked the idea—"

"She's jealous of you," George said for the umpteenth time. "Now will you believe me?"

"Yeah, okay," Nancy said with a modest shrug.

"What about Christy's sandwich?" Hawk asked. "Why did Randy do that?"

Nancy took a deep breath. "Christy overheard Randy negotiating the cougar sale on the phone. She was furious at what she saw as his betrayal of her. She threatened to go to the police. That was the phone call I overheard outside her office. After that, Randy went to her house, sneaked the greens into her sandwich, which she'd made earlier that day, and took her cougars away."

Bess took her last bite of waffle. "What was Christy doing at the zoo the other night?" she asked. "Was she meeting Randy or something?"

Nancy shook her head. "She wanted to find out the cougar buyer's name so she could tell it to the police. She thought Randy might have it on his Rolodex at work, but she couldn't get into the infirmary."

"And to think that Randy wanted to be a veterinarian!" Bess exclaimed. The thought caused them to change the subject.

After brunch the five friends strolled over to Katie's cage. As Nancy peered through the bars, Katie looked at her through half-closed eyes, while the four cubs nursed greedily.

"Katie's staring right at you, Nancy," George commented.

Katie opened her mouth and let out a contented sound. "Did you hear that?" Bess piped up. "Let me translate. She's saying 'All my thanks to Nancy Drew' in cougar language."

Nancy laughed. "Now, Bess, can you tell me how to say 'You're welcome'?"